BLOOD
WATER
PAINT

BLOOD
WATER
PAINT

JOY McCULLOUGH

THORNDIKE PRESS
A part of Gale, a Cengage Company

Farmington Hills, Mich • San Francisco • New York • Waterville, Maine
Meriden, Conn • Mason, Ohio • Chicago

TJ
LP

LIBRARY OF CONGRESS CIP DATA ON FILE.
CATALOGUING IN PUBLICATION FOR THIS BOOK
IS AVAILABLE FROM THE LIBRARY OF CONGRESS

ISBN-13: 978-1-4328-6683-9 (hardcover alk. paper)

Published in 2019 by arrangement with Dutton, an imprint of Penguin Publishing Group, a division of Penguin Random House LLC

Printed in Mexico
1 2 3 4 5 6 7 23 22 21 20 19

For Cordelia,
I want to know your story

PART I

PART I

1.

Everything begins from here:
the viewing point,

the place where you stand,
your eye level.

That single point on the horizon
where all other lines

                              converge.

2.

Sometimes when I breathe in
the linseed oil and turpentine
and roll the brush between my fingers

when I train my eyes
on what's ahead: my purpose,
and listen only to the rise and fall
of my own breath as I connect

      the brush to the paint to my
        breath to the canvas

I shut out the rest.

And then?
My father's rants
           tirades
               rages
over debts
       commissions
            jealousies

recede into the background,
underpainting
that I'll cover up
with strokes
of my own choosing.

I do not hear him
criticize technique, complain
I've strayed from his intent

remind me who the painter is.
It's funny how the painter's not:
      the one with pigment smeared
         into her skin
      the one whose body
      is as permanent a fixture
      in this studio as stool, palette,
         easel,
      the only one whose heart is flung
      across this canvas.

No: the painter merely signs his name

             and takes his gold.

3.

Gold could be the answer
to the Holy Child's curls.
Plain brown and he's no different
from my younger brothers
at our mother's breast.

I study my palette,
wonder how to blend
a luminescent glow.
I do not notice Father
stalking toward me
till he flings his arm
toward the easel,
knocks a crock of brushes
to the floor.

I can't tell who it's supposed to be!

I sit back, assess
the angle of the Virgin Mary's arm
as she cradles her holy child.

Little wonder
you don't recognize them.
When was the last time
you accompanied us to Mass?

Don't get smart with me.

My father spits his words,
flecks of rage arcing over my head
and slapping baby Jesus on the cheek.

If your brothers showed any
promise —

— They don't.

I ought to paint
with lighter strokes.
Dwelling on
my talentless brothers
only incites him.
They limit his prospects,
leaving him
for his apprentice
nothing but
a seventeen-year-old girl.

13

4.

Seventeen giulios
will buy a certain amount
of bread when Tuzia
hobbles to market,
clutching the purse
between gnarled fingers.

When she sends me, though,
if I duck my chin,
peer up through fluttered lashes,
give a twinkling smile
to Piero the baker
while my fingers brush his,
seventeen giulios
can suddenly buy
several more loaves
than they did before.

The bread is paid for
by commissions
I complete and so

my father does not dispute
a girl apprentice.

(Dispute? No.
Show gratitude? Well.)

5.

*What is that ridiculous
expression on her face?*

I redirect my eye
to the Madonna's face.
He is my teacher, after all,
for what he's worth
                (not much).
A mediocre painter,
Orazio Gentileschi,
but from time to time
he drops a seed
I can nurture
into something more fruitful
than he's ever imagined.

Or sometimes
what he says
is wrong,
but if I pinpoint
why he said it,

16

I learn.

This is such a time.
Her face is not ridiculous.
She gazes at her child in adoration.
The baby may be holy king savior god
but to his mother
he is simply love.

She looks drunk.

I try to shake him off,
hike up my skirts
for ease of motion
to reach for my paints,
connect with the canvas.

What does he know
of motherly love?
Though if I am careless,
my mother's voice
in my imagination
will recede.

6.

Not even voice
but breath upon my neck,
the slightest whisper
if I concentrate,
reach out in hopes
I'll feel her reaching back.

She's there, but not.

My head tipped back,
gaze heavenward,
these dismal surroundings
fall away.

Nearly.

In a moment of madness
        (or clarity)
my ambition
burns a hole in the ceiling,
allows the light

a direct path to
my canvas.

But then Father's there,
my gaze snaps down.

> *Get downstairs.*
> *Potential buyers.*

And so I'm hustled
down the stairs
as loudmouthed men
ascend to fill the studio
       (my studio),
intent on courting favor
from the church
by flaunting pious art
to make up for
less-than-pious lives.

Two men pass
without a glance my way,
the third makes very sure

I feel his gaze.
No longer do I covet light.

I wish men
would decide
if women are heavenly
angels on high,
or earthbound sculptures
for their gardens.

But either way we're beauty
for consumption.

7.

Head out of the clouds, girl.
We're off to market.

Tuzia shoves
a basket into my arms.

I blink,
try to shake off
the weight of a gaze
I never welcomed
from a man
who now occupies
my studio, perhaps
even sits on my stool
as he ogles
my Madonna.

On our return, though,
Tuzia will weigh me down
with produce, beans, dried fish.

She says young arms
can better bear the weight,
but then I wonder:

Why not bring my brothers?

My thoughts wander
heavenward again
as I linger with my Madonna
— and her child
too small to understand
what she has sacrificed
to give him life —
while my feet trip along
the cobblestones
of Piazza di Santa Maria.

Piazzas, churches
named for a teenager
who gave life to the Christ.
Sculptures, paintings, frescoes
devoted to her holiness.
But the only thing about her
we remember:

she was a virgin.

We must stop by
the apothecary.
Your father needs
more linseed oil.

My father needs more linseed oil,
Prospective buyers need the studio.
The boys need figs and fritters,
sugared apples Tuzia buys for them
with coins
that should be mine.

But I'm not meant
to have desires at all.

8.

When I am wrenched from easel
to fulfill some menial task
just as easily completed
by one without the skill to paint,
I am determined to use the time
to my advantage.

If I must leave the studio
at least I'll notice every shade of green
that's blended through the trees
and how a crack divides
a cobblestone, ant brethren
stranded across a great divide.

These are things I must observe
if I'm to paint the world with truth.
And yet I am distracted from my
    purpose,
not by Tuzia's constant rambling,
but by my mother's voice,
more vivid in this place

than any shade of green.

I spiral down
through many years
until I do not only hear her voice;
I'm with my mother
on the way to market,
skipping through this very square.

The Piazza di Santa Maria's
octagonal fountain boasts
      four stone wolves,
        at watch for centuries.
I'm not certain
whether the beasts
are meant to protect
the Holy Mother
or remind her
of her place.

The fountain is undergoing renovation.
I want to stop, observe
the craftsmen as they chisel

the stone, but Mother yearns
to move along.

The baby's coming soon
        (I cast a wish toward heaven
        that I might finally have a sister)
and Mother's feet are swollen
from the weight
she bears.

Still, she says,
the sun beating down
on her aching back,

    You watch, my love, my life.
    This fountain
    in our little piazza
    will now be connected
    to the aqueduct
    Acqua Felice.
    This is progress,
    before your eyes.
    You watch.

Now she's dead.
I've seen no progress.
The stone wolves
remain fixed to earth.

The only thing
that's changed is
she's not here
to say

> *I see you*
> *hear you*
> *want to know*
> *your story.*

9.

Linseed oil?

Adds gloss and transparency to paints.

Drawbacks?

Can yellow and become brittle with age.

Father's boots clomp
across the floor
like elephants in
our attic studio.

Each time he barrels past
I brace the table
where I grind our pigments,
prevent them from tumbling
to the ground.

Alternatives?

Poppyseed oil or safflower oil.

I don't know how many times
I have to demonstrate
my superior
grasp of our trade.

> (Except I do: as many times as
> Father asks.)

I turn my head
from sour breath
as he looms over
        my shoulder
to peer into my mortar
at the pulverized vermilion.

> *Grind that finer.*
> *Turpentine comes*
> *from . . . ?*

I throw my shoulder into it,
more pressure than I need,
but the harsh scrape

of marble on marble
relieves an itch
I can't otherwise reach.

Turpentine, Artemisia!

I exhale too hard.
A bloodred cloud
of ground vermilion
balloons into the air.

Comes from —
I sneeze
— pine tree resin.

But we use . . . ?

Venice turpentine.

From the —

— larch tree.

I do not wait
for him to ask
what's next.
The sooner this is over
the sooner I can return
my eyes (my heart)
to the canvas.

Because it adds
to the stability
of the paint surface
and yellows very little.

He glares.
Not because I've left something out.
Because I haven't.

10.

The fumes
from Tuzia's onions
meet me on the stairs
as I descend, their tendrils
dancing into my senses,
catching hold and dragging me down
to whatever task
awaits.

The moment I step foot
inside the kitchen,
Tuzia plunks down
a bowl, skitters a knife
across the block of wood between us.

                              Chop.

I do not know the difference
between chop
          slice
          dice.

I do not care to know
but take some pleasure
in the blade I wield.

The onions needle
at my eyes, my nerves,
no matter how many layers peeled back,
the same relentless stinging.
        (No matter how skillful my
            painting,
        Father's incessant nagging.)
Somehow even more meddlesome:
my brothers darting
constantly through.

Serves Giulio right
when he burns his tongue
on a ladleful
of boiling stew
(but I'm the one
who cleans the mess
that splatters to the tile).

What they've been doing

all day long
I couldn't say.

They have no aptitude
for painting, but still
they could be taught
the business.
Father says
they do not have
the head for numbers
charm for clients
patience
cunning
fortitude.

Here's what they do have:
freedom.

11.

Once upon a time
I was a child,
not the woman
of the house.

Not so long ago
but long enough
the days of tugging
on my mother's skirts
in hopes of being lifted up
at every whim
are hazy round the edges,
like a shadow bleeding
into light.

It's hazy how,
her belly round
with brothers,
Mother still made room
for me to crawl
up on her lap

to hear a story
no one else would tell.

How she'd look down
and ask me what I thought
of Father's paintings,
listen to my answer.

It's hazy how
she made my father
laugh.
How when I'd startle
in the night she'd soothe me
with a tune
to chase away
the monsters.

It's hazy how
her last few weeks,
confined to bed,
the child inside
a greater weight
than those who came before,
and even when the child arrived

a sister, finally, cold and blue,

and fever dreams bled
into pain laced with delirium,
Prudentia Montone spent
the last of her strength
to burn into my mind
the tales of women
no one else would
think to tell.

Those stories
of a righteous woman,
her virtue questioned
through no fault of her own;
of a widow
with nothing left to lose . . .
No way to tell
where shadow ends
and light begins

but Mother was always
the light.

12.

Light dances on the child's curls
and whether Father sees
or not
the bond between the baby
and his mother is
perfection.

Twelve years
with my mother
were not enough
but I know how to paint the love,
the source of light.

The final touches that remain
would go unnoticed to an unskilled eye.
In truth, I could release her now.
A signature the final touch,

Orazio Gentileschi,
(never Artemisia)

the client would be satisfied,
and none would be the wiser.

But I would know
her arm is
                              not quite right.
It wraps around the baby,
yet still looks flat.

Father babbled out
some useless nonsense
when I tried to ask him
how to fix the problem.
I don't think
he understood
my question.
If he cannot see
the problem to begin with,
how could he ever solve it?

It's only a commission,
doesn't even bear my name.
But I'm not only painting the Madonna.

I'm building a ladder,
each new technique,
a rung.

13.

Every time my father shoos me
down the stairs
away from my studio,
each time he speaks to buyers
      as though I am not there,
each time they leer at me
      as I descend in seething fury,
my mother's stories
stoke the flames inside.

We mostly deal in Bible tales,
some portraits, ancient histories, myths.
But all the maestros
sign their names
to David, Adam, Moses.
Those who follow strive
to leave their mark as well.

I can paint a David — king or upstart
    boy,
but when I do

there's nothing of me
on the canvas.
Susanna, though, is different.

My mother never held a brush
but still composed
the boldest images
from the brightest colors
drawing the eye — the mind —
to what mattered most:

> the young woman
> stealing a moment
> of peace to wash
> away the day

> then her world,
> stained beyond repair.

Susanna and the Elders.

Father's made attempts at Susanna,
just like the other painters — men —

who think they have the right
to tell the story of a woman
always watched.

But one can't truly tell a story
unless they've lived it in their heart.

The longer I'm shuffled
in and out of the studio,
used for what I can offer,
not what I long to share,
the more certain I am
I can do Susanna justice.
I can do my mother justice.

I can have justice.

But I'm holding back
until I think
perhaps
my skills
can match
my heart.

14.

My arm cradles my palette,
rounded, three-dimensional.

I paint *alla prima* in my mind
exactly how it should look.

Why then can I not transpose
      the image in my mind
      the image of my flesh
onto the canvas?

I stare at the Madonna's
flat, flat arm so long
my eyes begin to blur.
I do not notice
the creak of stairs
      moan of door
        steps that cross
          the studio.

Or perhaps he does not enter

like a mortal man
but appears
fully formed
a miraculous apparition.

Then:
                    a breath
                    upon my cheek.

Not Father's breath.
I grope for hiked-up skirts,
fling endless, heavy layers
of propriety
toward my ankles.
I am a model Roman girl
(or I can play the part at least).

The man averts his eyes,
steps back to give me space,
as though he doesn't realize
his mere presence in this room
drives out all air.
He may as well

be pressed against me.

He did not mean to startle —
that much is clear.
And even now as I
        recover
        steady my breath
        check my skirts once more
his eyes are not on me
but on the canvas.

My name is Agostino Tassi.
And you are Artemisia.

PART II

PART II

Surrounded

Forget what you know of the woman in the garden, my darling girl. The woman bathing until two elders of her community happen upon her. Forget the way you've heard the story in the scriptures, or seen it on your father's canvas.

Listen, instead, to your mother. Listen when I tell you that Susanna did not ask to be given to a wealthy man before her elder sister was married. She did not ask for the beauty that attracted him. She did not ask for gold and jewels. To you these might seem like unimaginable luxuries. But beauty is a heavy crown.

So is womanhood.

A servant kneeling at her feet, caressing them with oil, cannot massage away Susanna's guilt. Those comforts cannot shield her from her sister's bitterness.

(I so hope this growing seed I bear will be a sister for you. Sisters share a bond unlike any other — thornier, but also tender, full of possibility.)

I do not mean to say Susanna's life is all a trial. She does not toil for her bread. Her husband does not strike her, and while a man should aim higher than that, Joaquim is truly a good man. Susanna loves him — she thinks. As much as any woman barely into womanhood can love the man who married her so long as she brought herds of goats and storehouses of grain to their union.

There are also the servants. It might seem odd to complain about those who bear the weight of a household. My back aches not only from the weight of the child I bear, but from all I must carry as a woman.

But Susanna is surrounded. Her ladies-in-waiting hang on every word, every breath, and her patience wears thin.

Even as she prepares to bathe, they are there. Watching, waiting. The walled garden is not so private with four other people testing the water, fussing over her robe, setting loose her hair.

Susanna has lived in her husband's home for months now. She has been patient. But there are many parts of her life in which she has no say, and this is one small hill on which she might take a stand. She decides that even if she causes offense, it will be worth the momentary peace she'll gain.

(If you remember nothing else of Susanna, remember how she speaks her truth. She knows it will cost her something. She's not aware yet quite how steep the cost will be, but still, she speaks her truth.)

She shrugs off the lady trying to remove her robe and says to her attendants, "I'd like to be alone, if you don't mind."

They mind. They will not say so, but their eyes betray a shock as deep as if she'd slit a throat before them.

From the corner, Susanna's sister huffs. "They're your servants," she sneers. "They're meant to be on hand if you need anything."

They are not precisely servants, though.

If they were, Susanna could bid them come and go as she pleased. No, these are ladies of a certain station, always groveling, hoping their proximity to a woman like Susanna will help them ascend.

They're not to be faulted for it, either. They simply wish to survive.

Susanna understands this. But still, she stands her ground. "Thank you, Rebecca, ladies. But I'm more than capable of bathing myself."

The women go, horrified, muttering among themselves as they file into the house.

Rebecca stays, imagining herself in a different category from the women Susanna just dismissed. And she is. But that doesn't mean Susanna wants her there, peering across the garden wall at the village beyond the olive grove.

"You should take more advantage of your station," Rebecca says. "When I have my own rich husband . . ."

And there it is, the root of all the tension since Susanna married Joaquim: it should have been Rebecca.

There is no satisfactory way for Susanna to respond. She'll only be stepping into Rebecca's trap. She decides she can bear Rebecca's presence, but she will not lower herself to argue.

Instead, she lowers herself to the flat, black rock by the shimmering water and dips her hand in. The temperature is perfect. From here, she can no longer see over the garden wall. No other world exists.

Except Rebecca is still there.

"You're so ungrateful," she persists. "Everything is always handed to beautiful, righteous Susanna. Imagine if you were living at home at my age. Then you'd see!"

Susanna has compassion for her sister, but they have had this conversation one too many times.

"I see I'll never be at peace unless I'm completely alone. You may go, too."

The hurt that flashes across Rebecca's face is real. But it's also a performance — for Susanna, for the ladies watching from the window, for Rebecca herself. She's always aware of the audience. (So is Susanna — the difference is, Susanna would rather not have an audience.)

"Are you dismissing your own sister like a common servant?" Rebecca doesn't wait for a response. She stalks toward the door, performing the dramatic exit she craved. She'll be happier there anyway, where she can play lady of the house and contemplate new reasons to complain.

But for now, my darling, Susanna bathes alone.

15.

My studio
has always been
the place I am
hands and heart,
eyes and mind.

Nothing else.

But now,
a stranger in my studio,
a man,
and I am more aware
of every inch of skin
than inch of canvas.

He doesn't look at me
but at my work,
my heart outside my body.

That look,
it's what I long for, fight for —

an audience,
and not just eyes,
but a mind that understands
the skill required —
and yet somehow
a surge of envy
grips my soul.

Envy! Of the Holy Mother!
Rendered by my own brush!
Surely I commit several damnable
sins even as I stand here, immobile.

He shifts his weight.
The moment he's poised
to turn his gaze on me,
my most fervent wish
is that he'll never stop
examining the Mother and Child
because I am not prepared
for what's to come.

My neck has flushed, I feel it;

that color travels down
a vast expanse — it's far too vast —
until it meets the bodice of my dress,
a shield but also constrictor
of my breasts, my breath,
I cannot breathe.

I must.
I'll never be the giggling girls
who huddle in the piazza
or lean out windows,
dropping notes to their beloveds.
More than once I've wondered
what it would be like
to have no more pressing cares
than whether my love
might pass beneath my window.
But I decided long ago what mattered.
Now this man has come for me.
Not in that way —
        I'm such a child!
And yet I cannot keep from
echoing his voice inside my head

as my name falls from his lips.
At the thought
my knees give way.

But Mr. Tassi's deep in contemplation,
doesn't pay me any mind.
Doesn't see me grope the air
for where to place my hands,
arrange my arms,
learn how to stand again.

I pick a focal point and breathe.
If I can learn
to paint with nothing
but my wits
then I can make it through
a conversation
with this stranger
in my studio.

16.

Agostino Tassi's
    thick, furrowed brows
    hover over pitch-black eyes
    fringed with lashes longer than
    the strands of my best paintbrush.

(Do I exaggerate?
Perhaps.
But I've been living
in a muted, neutral palette
and now the sun shines through
stained glass more vibrant
than Marcillat's
Life of the Virgin.)

His tousled hair nearly brushes
the slanted ceiling of this horrid studio.
His cheekbones are chiseled from marble
by a sculptor with no subtlety,
    but there's softness too.
He gazes at the canvas,

open to whatever it brings.

Suddenly I'm mortified
by these dismal surroundings.
He shifts his weight —
>   impressive weight, no delicate
>   artist, he,
>   a hum of power thrums through
>   his bones —
the floorboards creak.

The rich brocade
of his jacket is more valuable
than all my clothes combined.
So much finer than anything I own

and suddenly it's very clear
this man is from the outside world
a man I've never met
alone with me
inside my studio —

>   my father's studio.

As if in answer to the unasked question,
Signor Tassi wrenches his gaze
from my Madonna,
turns his charcoal eyes
upon my frazzled face,
no doubt smudged with
    pigment
    panic
    sweat —

Your father's kitchen girl
let me up.

17.

I once found mouse tracks
in the bread dough
and it's not uncommon
for flies to float
through our wine.

Tuzia's snores fill
the tiny room we share
so even when my mind
has slowed enough to sleep,
I can't.

In the corners,
great dustballs congregate,
accusing me of neglect
as woman of the house.

Her doughy bosom,
graying hair,
plump but muscled arms,
bring to mind a kindly woman,

affectionate, warm.
She's not.

But mostly:

Tuzia has made the choice
to leave me unaccompanied
in the studio
with a man.

Not father, brother.
Man.

And instead of urging him toward the
     door,
I wonder how I can make him stay.

18.

The canvas is blank.
He makes the first stroke.

> *Your father asked*
> *if I might take a look*
> *at your most recent work.*
> *He says you need help*
> *with perspective.*

Is he coming?

(Pause.)

> *He was dealing with*
> *debt collectors in the piazza.*

That's embarrassing.

> *I assume it is Orazio's debt,*
> *not yours?*

Yes, Signor Tassi.

He winks.
I flush.

> *Call me Tino.*

Oh, I couldn't.

He gauges my discomfort,
returns his gaze to my Madonna.
I wait for him to speak
but when I cannot stand
the silence any longer:

My father says
you've come to town
for the Quirinal Palace commission.

> *That's true.*
> *I expect your father's hoping*
> *I'll bring him in on the*
> *   commission*
> *more than he's hoping*

I'll teach you perspective.

Of course.

The arm's a bit flat.

He may be here as a connection,
but he's skilled.

*If my father were
any sort of artist
he could teach me himself.*

*You're a lucky girl,
that your father's willing
to have you
as apprentice.*

My tongue gropes for words,
redemption.

*You're not wrong,
by the way.*

His painting is shit.
Between us, of course.

A strangled bark
of laughter escapes.

Of course, Signor Tassi.

I'm not the only one
speaking out of turn.

He looks at me.
Through me.

    Tino, please.
    I meant that.

Really, I don't —

    It'll be our little secret.

It's no small secret,
to call him Tino.

Tino.

You see?

His smile fills the room
as though each wall is glass,
and ceilings too,
and this, the sunniest
spot in all of Rome.

*That wasn't so hard.
Roman society did not storm
the walls, drag us away
to be tortured.*

I'll tell you another secret.

What's that?

*There's a lot you can get
away with
when no one is watching.*

Carefree

Close your eyes, love.

See in that artist's mind of yours Susanna in her garden. Carefree, but only for a moment. Because, you see, you're not the only one watching her.

There are intruders lurking just out of reach. It seems inconceivable at first. She's in her private garden, her home. She's sent her ladies away. Why, then, would two men be leering over her wall, stealing what's rightfully hers?

They're not monsters, either. Not men you'd shrink away from on the street. On the contrary. They're men you'd see at Mass, who'd give you a polite nod while they greet your husband.

You can imagine having a husband,

can't you, darling?

The important thing to remember here is that these two men are leaders in their community. Handsome, even. Respected and wise. Entrusted with advising the highest levels of government.

Of course, they don't need to be respected leaders to have more power than Susanna. Any man who breathes has more power than a woman in her world — and our world, too. And these men who lurk on the other side of the wall, planning their attack on a woman who only thought to wash the day away, will crush her world to dust upon a whim.

This may shock you, for you are still young. But this should not surprise Susanna. Of course she'll startle when she realizes they're there, but upon reflection, she'll understand that she's a woman in a world where her father got a receipt of sale upon her wedding day. She is a thing to be used by men.

And you should realize, love, that even the simple act of a bath is potentially world-altering. But then, you never see the beast until he is upon you.

19.

I am a child learning
single-point perspective.
Perhaps next we shall
mix blue with red
and see what we discover!

Still, I consent.
I've never had
a proper teacher.
So I will be
a proper student.

I listen to Signor Tassi

Tino, I insist.

determined
to make the most
of his wisdom.

In single-point perspective

there's one vanishing point.
The place where all lines
parallel to the viewer
converge.

> *Just imagine:*
> *you're standing*
> *in the middle*
> *of a long, flat road,*
> *gazing as far as the eye can*
> *see.*

He's poised behind me,
pointing; one hand
rests on my shoulder,
the other stretches
out in front
of our bodies,
my heart thudding
so hard I may not hear
what he says next.

> *Somewhere, far out in the*
> *distance*

the two sides of the road
will come together
in one vanishing point.

They always come together,
those two lines.
Even if they're very
far apart to start.

We stand there for a moment, staring
down the length of his steady arm
side by side, breath in sync,
converged like the point
out on the horizon
where our two
lines have
become
one.

Trapped

One more story, love. Then we must slip into dreams.

Now where did we leave Susanna? Ah yes, her sister threw a tantrum. But that all melts away the moment Susanna dips her toe into the water.

(I do so wish this baby's tantrums might be calmed by a single drop of water. But do you know, the constant kicking, pushing, jockeying for the best position leads me to believe you'll have a sister soon enough. Your brothers never kicked this much. But you . . . oh, darling girl. Even from the start, you couldn't bear to be constrained.)

Susanna, too, is trapped. She endures it with more grace than you, but she is older. She understands the world she lives

74

in. She doesn't want to cause a scene. But if presented with a choice, she'd happily trade the rest of Joaquim's grand home — the painted tiles, carved archways, every last detail her sister pines for — for this private garden, this bit of bliss where the late afternoon sun beats down to warm the water where it pools.

Why should a little corner of the garden be so important to a woman like Susanna? A woman with a palatial home, and the finest garments. Because imagine it — if you live as she does, surrounded by endless people and their expectations, ones you cannot possibly live up to, you do not even want to live up to — that refuge might be the only place you are safe.

When Susanna's stripped off her robes and slipped into the blue, it no longer matters who her husband is. She can pretend her parents never handed her over like one of the prize goats that came along in the deal. That her sister never wept at the injustice, never slashed the robe she was to wear on her wedding night in retribution for something Susanna never wanted to begin with.

Sometimes, when she escapes to the

garden, she slips all the way under, lets the water close over the top of her head, and relishes the utter and absolute silence. The last time she tried that, though, she only enjoyed the silence for a few moments before hands clamped over her arms, yanked her back up, a reverse baptism. Gossiping maidservants fluttered around, congratulated themselves for saving her, scolded her for needing a savior.

Susanna did not need a savior.

She learned to swim in the river with her brothers when she was still young enough to steal a tunic and run about the village as a boy. She will not drown in a shallow pool. And trapped though she feels, Susanna would not choose to fill her lungs and make the silence permanent.

But there will be no convincing the ladies around her that she will not soon need saving again. Ever since that day, they have stuck to Susanna like honey dried into the fibers of her finest dress.

Some days Susanna pities them, the women who'll never stop grasping toward a station they'll never reach. But today is not one of those days.

Susanna is grown by the standards of her world, but in this moment, her youth shines through. She makes a face exactly like the one you make when you find greens upon your dinner plate, and casts it toward the window where she knows the women loom.

Then she holds her breath and sinks into obscurity.

20.

The water has grown cool
but the air upon my wet skin
is cooler still.
I sink deeper in the tub.

Tuzia promised
to bring more
boiling water.
But now she
oohs and aahs
as Giulio recites his lesson,
my bath forgotten.

My teeth begin to chatter.
I brace myself,
then stand,
gasp as the air hits my skin.
This is the moment
Tuzia chooses
to step into the room.

She grabs the length of cloth
I cannot reach
and flings it at me.

> *For decency's sake,*
> *cover yourself!*

No fawning maidservant
is Tuzia.
I step carefully from the tub,
dry myself, reach for my smock.

> *Must you always wear*
> *that ratty thing?*

If she is going to stand there,
scrutinize my every move,
then she can get her fill.

I turn and face her,
take the time to dry
my dripping hair
before I pull the smock
over my head.

I'm going to paint,
not meet the Pope.

Next up, my petticoats.
More layers than
the onions I will peel
before the day is through.

> *Signor Tassi will be here*
> *soon.*

I wait,
as though to say,
And so?

She cannot help herself:

> *Just because you*
> *are doing a man's work*
> *does not mean*
> *you need to look*
> *like a man.*

I shrug on my bodice,

lace it up.
I spend a moment
longer than usual
arranging the ruffles
of the smock
peeking out
from beneath.

At Tuzia's smirk
I cut her off.

*I don't entertain
a suitor. I learn
from one my father
wishes to exploit.*

21.

That burst of inspiration,
that sudden vision of the inner eye —
that's my first fire.

That's when I absolutely
must get the image
on paper — a sketch, a rough rendering
of the vision I see
perfectly in my mind.

When the first fire ignites,
there's no time to grind the colors
                    heat the oil
                            cut the linen
                                    stretch the canvas.

There's only time to capture it.

The thing that flows
from the charcoal to my scrap
of paper is nothing

that can be described
with words. Just an image
I can't even name.
Echoes of the tales
my mother used to tell.
Shadows of the places
where different colors come together.
Vanishing points.

Today, a girl
in a garden.
She's naked.
She's bathing.
Her face is unclear still —

        but wait.

It's clearer now,
calm and peaceful.
That's not quite right,
not for the end result,
I know, but this is now,
not then.

For at least a few more moments,
she doesn't know
what's waiting
behind that wall.

22.

My fingers burn
with desire to move
beyond sketches,
to place Susanna on the canvas
in her garden,
use what I've learned
to tell her story.

Before I can paint Susanna,
dual-point perspective's next.
My father's principal concern
for my next lesson, though,
is that I convince Tino
to bring him in
on the commission
at the palace.

Yet again
my work, my growth
is secondary to
my father's need.

23.

I do not paint in words.
Flattery, persuasion
are not colors on my palette.

Still it's not preposterous,
what I must ask.
There's no way
he can do it all himself —
      assistants are expected.
Yet Tino laughs as though
I'm joking until he sees my face.

*Haven't we agreed on the
quality
of Orazio's work?*

He waves at a nearby canvas,
the answer implied
in Father's uninspired strokes,
no different from the rest.

But Father will not continue
my lessons with Signor Tassi

if there is no hope
for his own advancement.

I've got a secret for you.

I'm not sure
what makes me say it
but Tino whirls around,
eyes dancing.

Is that so?

I take a step back,
but the words have flown.

*Papa's name would
be on the contract.*

I look him in the eye;
I must be clear.

But I would do the work.

The silence stretches
out between us.

Tino's mind connects
the pieces. It's not news,
surely —

    what's new is
    I've given it voice.

       Well.
       That sheds
       an entirely
       different light
       on the matter.

24.

New light
floods
the shadowy
attic of my mind.

Those ideas
shoved in storage
while I do my father's bidding
are dragged out,
considered
with budding hope
that I might have
not only the skill
but also an eager audience
if I should take the leap.

I will show him
what a daughter can do.

In my mind,
the woman in the bath

is no exalted doll.
She is all light and terror,
the Susanna I finally summon
from stories,
from first fire,
and finally,
from paint mixed with
my own sweat.

In my mind,
so close to the canvas,
she's not weighed down
by any artist's shortcomings.

My actual labor of the day
is trying to breathe life
into my father's version.

He's seen my sketches
all around and now
he's suddenly inspired
to tell her tale.

It doesn't matter.
He never listened
to my mother's stories, never bothered
to notice the fear of women.
He'll tell Susanna
just like all the others.

I can cover the flaws
in his talent,
but can do nothing
for the flaws
in his perception.

He shares prestigious company.
The way the masters paint her,
the men are monstrous,
creeping, loathsome beasts,
obvious villains.
Yet Susanna wears
a smile that says
she welcomes their attentions.

My mother knew
this wasn't right.

She knew the men
who paint Susanna
could not comprehend
a woman's feelings in that moment.

She knew I'd need Susanna
when I found myself
a woman in a world of men.

Girl as prey.

25.

Now that Tino's
given me the tools I need,
I'll paint my own Susanna.
I'll show these men
what I am made of, what
they've been missing.

As a child, I didn't understand
perspective.

But now I know that lines
do not exist in nature.
The line is only perceived,
a trick of the eye.
A line is nothing more
than the place where two areas
of color come together.

They crash into each other.
Those places where lines are perceived,
those are the areas of tension

and excitement. Two things colliding
are always the most interesting
things to watch.

Watched

Once upon a time, Susanna sank beneath the water, then rose renewed, prepared to play her role another day.

Not this time. This time Susanna pauses under the surface with the sudden knowledge eyes are watching. And not fretting maidservants. This is different.

(You've brushed up against this feeling, love. And as you grow you'll come to know it like the curve of your own breast. I wish it weren't so. I cannot change it; I can only arm you with knowledge.)

Susanna knows immediately she is being watched by eyes that have no place in her private garden. Her husband has not returned home from his travels. A gardener has not mistaken his schedule and stumbled through the gate.

She knows before she sees them who they are.

Not by name, of course. She is no prophetess, no Delphic sybil. She could never guess that two trusted elders of her community lurk behind the wall meant to keep her safe. Though she is young, Susanna is a married woman, pure and virtuous. There is no reason she should expect a man who is not her husband.

And yet she does. (Trust your instincts.)

She feels the weight of their gaze, the expectation, and in a split second she must decide: remain concealed beneath the water, knowing they'll still have access to her blurred form, or lunge for the robe hanging just out of reach, exposing herself as she opts for modesty.

(What would you do, love?)

Susanna lunges, feeling the oppression of their gaze on every inch of her skin. They do not move — their mere presence is threat enough. Instead, they watch, amused, as the creature they believe to be helpless struggles to tug linen over wet skin.

I don't want to spoil the story, darling

girl. But I must say this: Susanna is not helpless. What's more, she is nobody's creature.

When still they say nothing, Susanna speaks. Susanna, who has been taught over and over again that a woman must not speak unless spoken to, especially not to men of this stature.

"My husband is not at home," she says. Perhaps a foolish beginning, but who can blame her in a moment such as that? With time to formulate a careful statement, she might have said, "If you've come to see my husband, as you surely must have, since you can have no possible business with me, he is traveling. I'll let him know you stopped by."

But that is not what she said. She only confirmed what the men already knew. Her husband is not at home.

The taller one smiles. He is a widower Rebecca has her sights on, and Susanna wonders for a fleeting moment whether this will change her sister's designs at all.

Susanna risks a glance toward the windows. For Rebecca, for anyone. The windows didn't seem far away when she wanted to be left alone, but now the distance is endless. Are her ladies watching? They're always watching. Why don't they come out? Of all the times to respect Susanna's wishes.

Still the men say nothing. Susanna does not know what she would have them say, but their silence unnerves her even further.

"Is there something I can do for you, elders?"

She is only playing a role: hospitable woman. But when they finally speak, it is clear they have something very different in mind.

"Yes."

This man is like Joaquim's brother. He gave a toast at Susanna's wedding. They have shared meals, grieved loved ones.

He has a wife.

"You are expecting a child any day, aren't you, sir?" Susanna stutters, willing the robe to cover more of her skin. "Is Moriah feeling well?"

His clipped reply: "My wife is not your concern."

Again, Susanna has misspoken. But one is never taught how to carry on a conversation while two men stare at the wet robe plastering one's naked breasts. Whatever this is, it has to end.

"I will tell my husband you came by —"

"I don't think you will."

Susanna crosses her arms across her softest parts, more to contain her wildly racing pulse than to shield her form. Her body, they have seen. They may not have her heart.

The widower speaks again. "Take off your robe." It comes out almost like a gentle suggestion. It's not.

His mother died last spring.

He watches, careless, but something tells Susanna if she should not comply, he would be the one to rip her robe to shreds.

She opens her mouth to scream, but no sound comes out.

"They say you are a woman of great virtue. Such a woman would not refuse the orders of two respected elders."

Perhaps no sound comes out because

there's no one to hear. Joaquim is many days away. Susanna knows her maidservants feel no real loyalty. If they should hear her cry, see her compromised position, there's every chance they'd spread the word throughout the village how the virtuous Susanna spends her time when Joaquim is away.

Such accusations would mean death.

A stone wall separates Susanna from the intruders, but they could leap it in a second. Would they pursue her if she ran for the house? What then?

Perhaps it's not so much, what they ask. Only a glimpse, a second, a slice of skin. It would be over quickly. No one would have to know.

"The way your husband tells it, you are nothing if not subservient."

Susanna's stomach roils. Is it possible Joaquim discussed her in this way? Is that how all men talk?

But no. She knows her husband. She knows that just because many men use women like chattel, it does not mean her heart should grow hard.

She is resolved then. She will not do

what they're asking. There will be consequences, she knows. But there would be consequences to compliance, too. And anyhow, who is to say they would stop once they'd had their glimpse?

"You are not my husband."

This time, Susanna has said exactly what she meant to say. But there are consequences.

The two men are over the wall in the time it takes the sun to slip behind the clouds.

"Today I am your husband. Today I tell you to lower your robe, and if you deny me, the world will hear how the faithless wife of Joaquim cavorted in her garden with a man who was not her husband."

Susanna stands frozen. If she moves a hair to either side, she'll press up against one or the other.

"Would you really rather risk being stoned than lower your robe?" the other man says.

Susanna could lower her robe to these monsters who believe they can take whatever they want simply because they have the power. (I know I said they weren't

101

monsters. They are. You just can't tell at a glance. You never can.) But if she does what they ask, she will be dead tomorrow either way.

"Get out of my garden."

The shorter man, whose wife may be laboring to birth a child this very moment, lunges forward, clutches at Susanna's robe, and pulls.

There's more than one kind of strength. You know this already, love. If Susanna had to rely on her body, she would lose this battle. But Susanna pulls back with the strength of her heart, her mind, her force of will.

"Leave her," says the widower. "There will be more satisfaction in watching her die."

26.

My favorite palette knife
is gone.
It should be here,
on the far right edge
of the table where I keep
my brushes,
my paints.

That's where I left it.
And yet, somehow,
it's nowhere to be found.

I suppose it isn't fair
to fault my father,
though he's the one
who used it, moved it,
claimed it as his own
because of course he did.
That's just the way of things.
I beg and fight and scrape
for scraps while he just has to glance

upon a thing to make it
his.

27.

Father's gaze
lays claim
to palette knife and easel,
stretcher bars, apprentice.
They all belong to him.

And now as his eyes
burn into the back
of my head,
he expects me to jump,
do his bidding
without a word from him.
We both know
what he wants.

But I can play
his power games.
I sit and paint in shadows
while he waits.

Finally,

I stand,
cross the room
to the wrong side of the easel,
and meet his gaze
as I reach for the laces
of my bodice.

He shakes his head,
disgusted.

It's a Judith.
A new commission.
I only need a bit of leg.

28.

He calls me an advantage,
a thing the other painters
do not
possess.

That's true —
but I am not a thing.
Or a possession.

I hold this knowledge
in my heart
as I lift my skirt,
try to feel relief.
No nubile nude is Judith —
more a warrior
in my mother's telling.
(No one's asked me to paint a Judith.
But Judith wouldn't wait
to be asked. My mind sparks
with possibility.)

My father's version
of this Hebrew widow warrior
will be more kitten than lioness.
She'll have her skirts hiked up
as she takes (dainty) action.
It's just my calf.
He sees it every day
when I'm at work.

The difference is that now
                    he stares
                    analyzes
                    uses my body.

He does not like
for me to speak
when he is working
but:

Signor Tassi said
he will consider us
for the Quirinal.

Father's head jerks up.
I lose my grip;
my skirts slide down.

Us?

I told him I help out . . .

*I'm sure you did.
It seems I need you
to disrobe completely.*

Take Action

Listen, love.

There's a story I've been waiting to tell you, because I haven't wanted you to bear its weight just yet. There are many things I hope you'll never have to bear. But I know otherwise.

And this baby will not wait. If this birth should be my last . . .

So hush and listen. This is the story of Judith, who paces, half-dressed, consumed with outrage. You'll feel this outrage too one day. Perhaps you already have. It won't be for the same reasons. But you will rage, and be told you are too small, too weak, too feebleminded to be of use. You are not. Judith is not.

Her servant, always useful, sits and

mends a tear in her lady's shawl. Judith pretends not to hear the servant's muttering about how a young woman of Judith's station oughtn't rip her things like a child at play.

But childhood's murky when a girl is married off upon arrival of first blood. It's only when her lady rails like this, impassioned by injustice, not yet hardened to the world, that the servant is reminded how few years Judith has trod upon the earth.

"A few men speak for all, sentencing an entire village to death! I only know because I overheard. Everyone else, though? They sleep on, confident their leaders will protect them!"

And how else would Judith learn important news, unless she overhears? For this young woman drifts within a netherworld, without a man to anchor her. She ought to have returned to her family of origin upon the death of her husband and taken shelter under cover of her father's wing.

But even if the Assyrian army were not blocking all roads to Bethulia and out, Judith would be loath to throw herself upon the mercy of the father she challenged by marrying for love.

What's more, that love will bind her here to where she built a home with Malachi (or started to). She'll only leave if dragged away, and even then, she would not go quietly.

When Malachi left to investigate how close the Assyrians had come to Bethulia, Judith had no doubt Malachi would return.

When Malachi did not return with his fellow scout, Judith was certain he must have infiltrated Assyrian ranks, searched for a way to take out their captain and thereby halt the onward Assyrian march.

Finally, though, Judith faced the truth: Malachi would not return. Her only comfort was the thought that his death would serve a purpose. Bethulia's leaders would have to make a choice — flee or fight, it hardly mattered. As long as there was action. A reason for her heartbeat's death.

But now — now! — she's learned the only plan is hunker down and die. They could have done that without Malachi's sacrifice! Without Judith's sacrifice!

The servant pricks herself. A drop of blood blooms on the smooth pad of her finger. It's nothing. The servant would continue with her labors if she weren't concerned with staining the dress. But Judith swoops in as though Abra has been stabbed. She dabs the blood away with the hem of her skirt.

Abra sighs. One more stain to remove.

"Are you listening to me, Abra?"

The servant whistles the tune Judith's mother used to sing before Judith left for Malachi's village, taking with her only Abra, her righteous anger, and her love.

Judith stills Abra's hands, meets her eyes. "I know you heard me."

Abra doesn't have so many years on Judith. She's more older sister than wizened aunt. But no matter her age, she'll always be a servant.

"The Assyrians. I heard. And what business is it of ours?" Abra resumes her stitching as Judith resumes her rant. The pinprick of a moment before is forgotten as a much deeper stab of worry slices through Abra's heart. Judith isn't only outraged. Judith is planning something. There are things she can do, as a woman, Judith insists, that no man would think of, much less pull off.

When Judith finally takes a breath, Abra sets aside her mending. "Leave me out of it."

Perhaps the world has taught Abra she has nothing to offer but mending, cooking, cleaning. But Judith must do this thing that's only just beginning to take shape in her mind. Because she is not small. She is not weak. She will never, ever be feebleminded.

And above all, she is outraged.

The world will tell you not to be outraged, love. They will tell you to sit quietly, be kind. Be a lady.

And when they do? Be Judith instead.

29.

No matter
how many layers
of paint pile on,
I will always be
the sketch beneath.
Useful, even crucial,
but never what's
admired by the world.

If Father gave me leave
I'd fly away from here,
gone before he'd rinsed
the charcoal from his hands.

But where to go?
No answer to that
question, no point
in even asking.
Instead I pull out my Susanna,
the one I've hidden from my father
for fear his criticisms will dissuade me.

If one of the elders
leering at Susanna
should bear a slight resemblance
to Orazio Gentileschi
as he leers at a young woman's form,

  that's just
   a trick of the eye.

If the viewer sees a spark
inside Susanna's fear,
a hint she may be capable
of more than any man
has ever dreamed,
the faintest whisper
that at any moment
she might risk everything
to whirl around
and stare them in the eye,

  that's just
   a flight of fancy.

116

30.

i.

Why so blue?

Susanna pulses
through me
so entirely
I do not feel
the
        world
tilting
until a hand
rests on my shoulder.

Artemisia, why so blue?

I allow my heart to surge
at Tino's voice, concern.
One man, finally
who is not here

to use me.
But I do not
let him see
my pleasure.
Instead I stare, petulant,
at the canvas before me.

Do you have
another suggestion
for the sky?

> *I meant your temperament,*
> *my dear.*
> *When you paint,*
> *you glow.*
> *You radiate like the sun.*

And there,
he's done it.
Hoisted me out
of the depths,
turned me
on my head
again. I fight a smile.

I'm not blue.

*You are positively
cerulean.*

I consider him,
his face a blank canvas,
my next words
the paint.
But he is here
to be my teacher,
not my confidant.

I pick up the brush,
consider Susanna.
She's naked, too.

It's my father.

Tino's movement stutters.

*Truly? He bears
an uncanny resemblance
to Susanna in the garden.*

I meant —

> *You are remarkable,*
> *to have survived*
> *your lout of a father*
> *this long with such grace.*

He turns to Susanna.

> *If Orazio cannot see*
> *what you are doing here,*
> *cannot understand*
> *the risk you take when you*
> *paint Susanna in a new*
>   *light,*
> *then do something*
> *for me.*

Anything.

> *Cast him out of your mind.*
> *He's your father, yes.*
> *But you are the artist in this*
>   *house.*

120

You want to experiment?
Try something your father
doesn't approve of?
You trust your heart.

He speaks of my Susanna,
how I'm trying to capture
her fear
rather than
her beauty.
How I've made her
attackers handsome
                wise
                respected,
rather than vulgar
and obvious.

He understands!

ii.

Trust your heart,
he says, but his words

make me want to reach
deep inside for that piece of me that
    trusts,
dusty, unused
since my mother's death,
and hand it over,
rust and all.

My father hasn't seen
this Susanna.

I watch Tino
take this in.
He turns, waits,
like nothing is more important
or more pressing in his day.

I tire of being his model.

His brow wrinkles,
confusion blurs
his usual certainty.
Until finally:

Ah.

I don't mean
to pour myself
out before him
and yet.

If he'd let me do the painting myself it
    would be
better than his clumsy efforts
to reproduce my form.

> *From what I understand,*
> *you do most of the painting*
> *anyway.*

And yet he insists on the nudes.

iii.

His face falls
into shadow,
a Caravaggio
without the light.
I've overstepped.

For all our jokes,
familiarity,
I never should have —

Your father . . . ?

He takes a paintbrush
from my workspace,
turns it over
in his hands.

I step closer.
We've stood
this close before,
but always with
our gazes trained
on the canvas.
Now we're
face to face,
heart to heart.

Your father . . .

The paintbrush snaps.
I startle at the crack.
His eyes meet mine,
shift from rage
        to soothing silk.

I'm sorry,
my darling.
I must —
Your father's never . . . ?

My skin crawls.
My father's never laid
a hand on me.
It's true, he orders me to strip,
to be his model
                puppet
                    slave
but I am not — at least — that.

I tear my eyes
from Tino's,
mumble to the floor:

125

No.

And then
    (I did not think it possible)
Tino draws yet closer.

> *Good.*
> *If anyone ever hurt you . . .*

He drops the broken brush,
grinds the pieces
to splinters
beneath his boot.

I lift my eyes to meet his,
grope for words.
For all the men
who populate
my world, there's never been a one
who wished to be
my champion.

I can survive, a solitary creature.

I have thus far.
But just the thought that someone else
might care what fate befalls me —
              it changes everything.

His fingers worry
the lining
of his blouse.

> *But then,*
> *you do not need*
> *me to play*
> *the older brother.*

Some force compels me forward —
              not my will, not his.
I stand so near
I see the very brushstrokes
of each eyebrow,
the unsubtle scrapes
of the sculptor
who formed his jaw.

So don't.

Inhale.
Exhale.
And then his lips
are one with mine.

PART III

PART III

31.

The house is a still life.
Except, perhaps, for the mice
no doubt scampering
through the pantry,
all is motionless.

Father's returned from his revelries,
drunk on all he gets out there
he cannot find in here
and dead to the world
until he must wake
to face his disappointment.
Tuzia's sculpted from marble
on the cot next to mine
(though not so silent).
The boys float through the dreams of
    those
who'll never have to fight to be heard.

I slip from bed
to studio

as silent as the mice.
We thieves in the night
steal what we must
when no one is watching.

The candles lit,
I search behind old canvases
and stretching bars until I find
my prize: a dusty mirror,
once my mother's and
last in use when time and again
I sketched my own face,
working out proportions
my father couldn't explain.

His grasp on female form —
a woman's body —
is even less precise.
But Susanna deserves better
than a man's idea
of what a woman should be.

I set the mirror on the easel,

listen again for footsteps, judgment.
Then, satisfied I am alone,
expose a shoulder to the air.

32.

Reflected in the looking glass,
neck curves into shoulder,
one shade blends into another.
As I lean closer, the glass reveals
a constellation of freckles
I've never noticed.

Emboldened by discovery
I let the fabric pool around my waist.
The midnight air
sends shivers up my spine.
My nipples tighten
against the creeping draft.

Even the greatest painters
portray a breast as though
it is one thing and then another:
a tiny, perfect drop of pigment
atop a milky dome.

But even in the guttering candle's light

I see something different,
more complex.
All around the pinkest tip
the color pools and fades
by gradual shades
into my ivory skin.

My fingers wander up, explore.
A breast rests in each palm,
the weight surprising.
The way men paint them
I might have thought
they'd float away
if they weren't tethered
to my earthly flesh.

I lean to the side,
      Susanna cringing from the elders'
        gaze.
In my mother's mirror,
my breasts follow.
They're not half spheres, unyielding,
behaving how a man believes they
    ought.

They shift and change,
they're form and function, and
they're mine.

33.

Back in my cramped room,
beneath my sheets,
I know I should sleep.
But my mind hums.
My hands don't stop exploring.

How have I lived this long
with my own body
in darkness?

The disconnect of men
to women's bodies
stands to reason.
They'd have to care enough
to see the other as a subject
worthy of their earnest study.
My own oblivion horrifies me more.
I've been here all along
but somehow not.

And now there's Agostino.

I can't pretend
these new discoveries
are solely for the sake of art.
Though every time he's near
it feels like brushstrokes
on a canvas, light, provoking,
transforming me to something new.

My fingers flutter lower
toward the pulse
I've steadfastly avoided.

Until now.

34.

When Tuzia grunts
to rouse me,
I startle from
the most delicious dream,

then hide under
my blanket, ashamed
of what she'd think
if she could read
my mind.

If Mother were here
would I tell her
how I woke heart pounding,
skin ablaze, ask eager questions,
drink up every answer?

Instead, there's only Tuzia.

We'll take a carriage to Mass.

35.

My cheeks still flame
inside the carriage
as we jolt along
the cobblestones,
      a hired ride
      our luxury
      when Father's been out
      drinking late
      and does not come to Mass,
      so Tuzia shames him
      into paying for our fare.

We've only just turned
onto Via della Lungara
when the carriage stops,
nowhere near our parish.
Tuzia leans forward,
puffed with temporary power
of being served
and not the servant.

We say our Mass
at San Giovanni.
Why have we stopped?

You've room for more.

The voice is not
our carriage driver's.

Tino! I exclaim
and if I thought
I'd flushed before
my face must now
be carmine red.

What nerve (of his!)
to flag our carriage down
as we are on the way to Mass!
What nerve (of mine!)
to call him by his name
as though we are united!

Tuzia's eyes cannot decide
if they should glare at me
or at our interloper.

Tino makes a move
to climb inside our carriage —
a violation of the rules
of decency, our code, our social order.

A moment's hesitation

    — I should not touch him
    as though we're so familiar
    but neither do I see another way
    to stop him so —

my hand shoots out
and grabs his forearm.
I feel his muscle, power, spark
and drop him as the fire
of my nighttime discoveries
jolts through my mind.

You must not join us,
sir.

I've never called him sir before.
I try to tell him
with a glare
what I cannot say plainly.

> (If you should
> push your charm
> out here in view
> of all of Rome
> you risk my father's wrath
> and never seeing me again.
>
> If you should
> bid me sit, ignore
> the lands I've only just
> discovered in the dead
> of night, my knees
> pressed close together, tight,
> you risk my own implosion.)

I only meant to go to Mass.

A flood of meaning
flows through his own
amused gaze.

Tuzia huffs.

I watch a calculation
pass across the charmer's face.
Tuzia is a servant.
Never has she dined
with cardinals, princes.
She has no talents
that could cast a spell
upon a Pope
like some among us.
Yet she is the key
to what he wants.

Agostino inclines his head.

My apologies.

But as we have a chaperone
of such esteem,
surely we can ride
together? A woman like
          yourself
would never allow
dishonor to fall upon
her charge.

I wait for Tuzia's scoff.
Instead she shrinks into herself,
gives the smallest
hint of smile.

We do not wish to be
uncharitable, good sir.

And then to me, she says,

Make room
for Signor Tassi.

36.

Firewood scrapes my arms
as I haul it to the still-dark kitchen
before my brothers stir,
demand their breakfast.
I barely feel the weight, though.
It's nothing to the weight
of Tino, ever in my thoughts.

No longer am I painting
every moment that I breathe.
Now attention wanders,
senses rebel,
focus is a point on the horizon
far too distant to identify.

I drag myself up to the studio,
not thinking forward
to what I plan to paint,
but backward to what Tino said
when last I saw him.

Like when we pulled up
to San Giovanni,
he leapt out of the carriage,
winked,
and said,

>   *Now you'll have*
>   *something to confess.*

I force him from my mind.
At least I force him
to the background.

He will not consume
my every thought.
I am a painter.
I will paint.

37.

I've only just begun
to feel the flow
of heart to canvas
when boots come clomping
up the stairs.

Tino bursts into the room,
a hurricane of energy
that just might knock
the brush from my hand.

I have it!

He knows full well
he's interrupted
but lacks the tiniest hint
of remorse in his twinkling eyes.

I make a show of setting down
my brush, my palette,
my plans for the afternoon.

You have
the terrible habit
of bursting in here
like a thunderclap.

> *Are thunderstorms not*
> *thrilling?*

You have my attention.

I push my skirts down to my ankles
and turn away from the canvas.
(Only for Tino
do I turn away
from the canvas.)

What is it?

> *The answer*
> *to all*
> *your problems.*

I snort,
distinctly unladylike.

Tino stretches out his arm,
inviting me to take his hands.
I hold mine up to show:
                    they're covered in paint.
He scowls, lunges forward,
pulls me to standing by my waist.
I mean to focus on his words
but his fingers linger.

The answer to all your
problems,
and a fair few of mine.

We stand so close
I could time my breaths
to his if I needed a guide.
I might.

But Tino puts
some distance
between us,
looks me squarely in the eye —

Your father

150

                        does not
                        value your skills.

This is not news.
I wait.

                        I am falling behind
                        on the Quirinal commission.

My breath catches.
I do not wish
to be the reason
his career falls flat.

I'm sorry.

                        You should be!

He points an accusing finger,
but his eyes dance again.

                        Through your fault entirely
                        I am captivated by you,

at all hours of the day,
when I ought to be chained
to my easel doing the
bidding
of the scandalously wealthy.

I can breathe again,
but only just.

I thought you had
a point somewhere?

Ah yes!

He holds up a triumphant finger: one.

Horrid father!

And a second.

Pressing responsibilities . . .

He trails off,
lost for his third point,

gazes around.

If I were to paint Tino's portrait
I'd have to decide:

>   Portray the angles of his jaw,
>   the fire in his gaze, the pure,
>   absolute beauty.

>   Or choose, instead,
>   the gleeful smile, the dancing eyes,
>   the clown whose day is not complete
>   until he's put a smile on my face.

>>   *Oh yes! The third thing:*
>>   *dreary studio.*
>>   *You're working*
>>   *in a dungeon, darling.*
>>   *Even you cannot*
>>   *illuminate it.*

I turn back to the canvas,
so he might not see

the flush upon my cheeks.
Thrilled at darling,
mortified at dreary.
We've discussed the studio before.
There's nothing I can do.
And yet I'm still ashamed.

Then he's behind me,
warm hands on my shoulders,
breath against my cheek,
setting me ablaze.

I think you'd enjoy my
studio.
Much more natural light
than this one.

Prepare

I'm going to blow out the candle now, darling. But you mustn't be afraid. You make your own light. And even when I've gone to sleep, you'll have my stories, yes?

When I wake up frightened, I think on Judith — also afraid, in the dark, very nearly alone, but not completely. Judith surveys the room, lit only by flickering candlelight. For the first time since Malachi's death, her heart is moved to action, to purpose, to hope.

"Pack that loaf of bread by the hearth. And get a jug of wine."

Clear, tangible actions lift the weight that has pressed down upon her heart every second since she became a widow. In this moment, she does not need to ponder who she is without Malachi or where she will go from here. She only needs to pack the necessary items. And what else will she and Abra need, besides their wits, and more courage than they've ever had to summon?

Abra sighs. "It's a long way to travel with heavy provisions. If they don't kill us, I'm sure they'll feed us."

It isn't that Judith doesn't understand where Abra is coming from. Judith's plans are outrageous, by any measure. Dangerous. Almost guaranteed to end in death. That's why Judith makes clear that her faithful maidservant is not required to accompany her.

Judith, though, has no choice in the matter. She must do this for Malachi, and all young lovers barely beginning their lives together, so others will not be wrenched apart by swords and greed and military might.

"You think I'm rushing off in the heat of passion. But this is me, making sure to be prepared. Isn't that wise?"

Abra scoffs as she shoves the bread into a basket. "You're dreaming of being a hero."

(And do you know, my love, there's nothing wrong with that.)

Judith slams the jug of wine onto the table with so much force she checks to see it hasn't cracked before she carries on.

"My husband's dead, Abra. The bricks of our home were not yet dry when they sent him out to keep our village safe. And now his sacrifice will mean nothing — unless I act."

"I didn't mean —"

"I know what you meant. I know what they'll say. 'That girl and her temper.' For I'm a little girl when they want to belittle me, a woman when they want me to bear a child. But my womb will be no use to anyone if all Bethulia perishes beneath Assyrian swords."

"Your womb will also be useless if you are killed." Abra shrugs. "Your womb is of little interest to me either way. But I'm somewhat fond of how you prattle on."

Abra doesn't always mind her station. But that's what Judith loves about her. Abra challenges her right up until she says, "Yes, ma'am."

Judith finds her heaviest cloak and motions for Abra to fetch hers.

Abra stares back in her simple, tattered tunic. "This is all I have."

Judith despises feeling foolish. But of course that's all Abra has. She is a servant, even though most of the time, Judith thinks of her as just another woman, struggling through.

"You'll take my cloak, then," she says, ashamed she hasn't paid better attention to Abra's needs.

Abra grins. "Already playing the hero?"

Judith fastens the cloak around her servant's shoulders. "If you're not careful, I'll leave you with the Assyrians. Now: this is your last chance. I won't order you to come."

There is a moment's hesitation, during which Judith fights against the panic that she might set out to do this thing alone, without the only person who can always steady her hand.

But Abra smiles again — not so wide this time, but true. "What?" she says. "And miss my share of the hero's welcome?"

With that, there are no more words to

be said. Judith hands the basket to Abra, bearing the weight of the wine jug herself. Then the two women slip out into the night and beyond their city's walls.

38.

Susanna should not be smuggled
like a stolen treasure
unfit for light of day.
And so I leave
my painting out

     exposed

when Father mounts the stairs.

I almost hope for praise
(portrait of
a little girl
as pride and joy)
but all he says is,

> *You're not doing
> what I asked you.
> Why?*

I do not say:

Because so far today
like every other day
    I've made (your) breakfast
    painted (your) commissions
    hung (your) laundry
    sketched (your) projects
    made (your) lunch
with never a second
for my own work?
Because I might have a moment
to consider my own work
if the menial tasks
were left to you,
who cannot paint
with any heart at all?

Instead:

I'm trying something new.
Tino saw the promise —

      You may be Signor Tassi's
          student
      but you are not

his daughter
and this is not
his studio.

No, but if I left
for his studio . . .

How would my father
feel if those words
fell from my lips?

Perhaps relieved.
I would be off his hands.
He would like to see me married,
someone else's yoke.
And yet without me,
how would he get by?

I'll boil the glue
before the day is over.

                    You'll do it now.
                    You cannot shirk

the less appealing
aspects of our craft,
simply because you think
them beneath you.

I could recite
his next words
by heart
but that will only
make the lecture
        longer.

There is no glory
in scraping
boiled rabbit hide
across your canvas.
But there is a better
finished product.
Grinding the pigments
not to your liking?
You must prefer
a gritty paint.
These are your options:

*You'll cook
and sew
and wipe a baby's ass*

*or you'll do what I say
when I say to do it.*

*No one else
is going to teach you
how to paint.*

39.

No one else
is going to inhale
the fumes of boiling
rabbit hide, or strain
the putrid chunks until
they're fit to smear across a canvas.

No one else
is going to haul
the cauldron full
of finished glue,
a witch's brew
from kitchen up to studio.

But I'm the witch,
a girl transforming
one thing to another without
an explanation for the wonders
that appear upon her canvas.

It must be sorcery.

Muscles screaming
as I reach the top,
I take a breath
and rest my head
against the wall,
careful not to burn
my hand against
the scalding iron at my side.

I've grown accustomed
to the lack of light
inside our studio.
But from this angle
of fatigue a ray
slants through
the window
to bounce across the surface
of the foul, gelatinous
potion I've just brewed.

Beneath the light, it's a golden sea,
tranquil but for the slightest breeze.
A place where magic hums

beneath the surface, mermaids,
water sprites, and queens
of gleaming realms.

The only spell
cast by natural light
illuminating what it finds.

In Tino's studio,
the natural light
just might find me.

40.

And yet in
his studio
he'd always be
the brighter light,
and I, reflecting
off him,
could never
shine so bright.

But still I'd shine.

41.

I've never seen inside
his studio.
But there are many things
a woman never sees
until she's joined unto a man.

42.

I replay
our last conversation
again and again and again,
a series of sketches
that never seem
to take shape
in a final
form.

Sketch:
Tino proposes
we share a studio.

Sketch:
Tino chooses me,
offers what he's never
offered to another.

Sketch:
I am chosen.
Not mere convenience,

scraping by.

Sketch:
Tino believes
I might inspire,
even teach him
what I know,
what he cannot.

Sketch:
I lose control
of proper speech
and fluster
bluster
muster up
no words at all
before my father
interrupts us.

43.

There is no sketching
what I'll say
when next he comes.

At the sound of his approach
I organize my brushes,
as though that will make
order of my jumbled thoughts.

He doesn't bring it up,
gets straight to work,
shows me where
I need more shade.

When I am past pretending
I care at all for shadows,
I adopt a teasing voice —
one I'd never use
if anyone were listening.

(There's a lot

you can get away with
when no one else is watching.)

I've been thinking
about what you said
last time.

I almost thought he'd forgotten,
or worse, I'd imagined
what he offered.
But no, at my words
he transfigures
before my eyes.

    I've thought of nothing else.

Truly?

    Look what you've accomplished
    in this horrid space.

To emphasize his point,
he twirls around,

arms outstretched,
nearly knocks
the easel over.
We both lunge to right it,
laughing.

> *Imagine what you*
> *would accomplish in my studio.*

I have an excellent imagination.
Yet I can't imagine
the great Agostino
would share a studio
with anyone.

He laughs, a boisterous thing
that bounces off the walls.

> *You think me arrogant.*

His hands encircle my waist.

> *And you're not incorrect.*

The tip of his nose
brushes mine.

> *But the things we could do*
> *together!*

Marriage
is the only possible
reason he could utter
those words — there is no other option.
My father ignored propriety
by teaching me to paint.
But Tino knows
I could not share
an outside studio, unmarried.

Do you mean — ?

He twirls me around,
creates a music
only we two can hear.

> *And if you shared my studio . . .*

I wait, heart
in my throat.
This is the missing color
I've never managed to blend,
never thought possible
from the choices on my palette —

> Let us just say:
> I would make better use
> of my live model
> than your father does.

44.

The Holy Mother
cradles her son's lifeless body.
Greedy Tarquin
grips the terrified Lucretia.
Hands on bodies
have no in-between.

Love
or possession.

I have been such a fool.

His arms are still around me.
Possession.

    I'm torn between
    the need to scream
    and grab my brush
    to finally get Susanna right.
    This is the moment
    we're truly one.

I disentangle
from Tino's grip,
stumble back,
grope for a brush
I do not find.

Have I shocked you?

Anyone
would be shocked
by that.

He draws near again — too near.

But surely not my cerulean
    one.
Anyhow, cerulean
is not your color.
I would paint you in
cream and chestnut,
rose and —

His hands have reached
beneath my skirts

and travel up my legs.
My nighttime explorations
turned to nightmares.
I wrench myself away.

Tino!
I'm saying no!

He blinks.
I'm not behaving
like his smitten girl
devoted student,
flirt and stroker of his ego.
I have a mind
        a will
        a vote.

He straightens up,
runs fingers through wild hair.

        Very well.

His eyes shift

to my canvas.

*Your shading is extremely
poor.
I doubt even I can fix it.*

45.

First I mix the oil
with hot water,
taking extra care
not to scald myself.

       I have been such a fool.

If I burn my hands
I'll only have myself
to blame.

I shake the oil and water then wait
for the liquids to separate.

       I built up hopes on nothing.

The oil rises as it should —
some elements of craft are art
but this is science.
It can be relied upon
to do what is expected.

He never truly wanted me.

I peer carefully
into the mixture of oil and water,
making sure the impurities
settle
at the bottom.

Not as an artist or a wife.

My father rails
about the process,
preparation.
And this is where he's right:
if there are impurities in the oil,
the painting will be ruined.

But nothing has really changed.

Next I remove the oil,
wash it in clean water.
(Susanna at the bath)
Once it is exposed,

the air will form a film
and so it must be stirred.

I'm only back where I started.

46.

A Susanna's never terrified.

Father told me so
when finally he
took the time to look.

The men who've painted
her a million times before
will always see her through
distorted lenses of their sex.
But I know
   what it is to be watched,
   to be leered at
   what it is to be a thing.

The only thing Father understands:
  my Susanna's different.
She's raw but skillful
— a tempting novelty —
and just might fetch a handsome sum.

(Everything produced
by this studio
is his property, after all.
Including the apprentice.)

And so he ushers
men into my inner sanctum,
to talk about my work
as though I am not there.
To value it, and me.
           (Evaluation: worthless.)
Word on the street: I didn't paint it.
A girl my age could never
accomplish such a thing.
They say it's from his hand,
           his brush,
                    his mind.

They call me words enough
to fill a book I cannot read.
I know the words, though —
words they hurl at any woman
foolhardy to force herself
into a world of men.

My father claims
to give me credit,
but I am never in the room
and my faith in men
is all dried up.

He says I shouldn't bother
with talk of the street.
After all, I know the truth.
What else matters?

What an interesting question,
coming from Father.
Wouldn't it be convenient
if I stayed forever locked here,

turning my head
as he signs his name
to my work, never caring
if anyone knows
who actually bled
onto the canvas?

47.

Tino lurches through the door
all stumbling boots and flailing arms.
No hint of smooth sophistication,
no wooing charm.
I wasn't sure
he would return
since I spurned his offer
      (such an offer).
Now relief and irritation
do battle in my heart.

            She had it coming.

He staggers closer,
nearly knocks Susanna
off the easel.

            Look at her
            on display,
            the tease.

This battle's not
just in my heart.
I spread my arms, shield Susanna
from yet another man
consumed by greed,
crazed with power.

What's wrong with you?

I ask, though any fool
could smell it on his breath.

*Students who never learn,
to start.*

Though he is drunk,
perhaps he simply needs reminding.
I flutter lashes,
become Susanna made by men.

*What happened to
your cerulean one?*

I don't know.

Lilting charm was not the answer.

You tell me.

This is about the commission.
It must be.
He's fallen behind.
But I could still help —

If you bring me on now, I —

He pushes past me;
I tumble off my stool.
He did not mean to shove
me down, but neither does he stop
to help me up.
He flings a hand
at my Susanna.

What is this shit?
Have I taught you nothing?
All planes must be
  perpendicular
or parallel to you in order

I let out a stream
of the foulest words
I've heard in this studio,
as I scramble to my feet,
right my stool, place myself
in the path of his rage
to protect Susanna.
Somehow that seems
the most important thing.

Oh-ho!

He laughs, a fleck of spittle
landing on my cheek.

*Look who's learned
a thing or two
in her father's house!*

He knocked me off a stool
    — a girl, a student —

and I'm the one who's vulgar?
I shake my head and turn away.
Deliver me from drunken men, I pray.

I face Susanna.
I'm standing far too close
to see her with perspective
but I pretend to study her,
wait for him to take his drunken rage
to someone else who cares.
(I care.
I care about Susanna more.)

You're drunk,
I'm working.
Come back
when you can
teach me something.

Instead of leaving, he sidles closer,
his breath crowding my cheek,
hands on my waist.

If I wait it out, he'll go.
I learned this as a child:

> When boys pull your hair,
> it means they like you.
> Just ignore them.

But I can't stop my heart
from hammering in my chest
as his hands slide higher,
hover just beneath my breasts.

Tears spring to my eyes.
But still I cannot let him see
he's reached inside me,
yanked hard on something soft and
tender.

I'm done being your pupil.

Ah, but my darling girl.

His breath is heavy in my ears,
his hands clamp down and squeeze.

> *There's plenty we could*
> *teach each other.*

I twist out of his grasp,
unable to feign calm
a moment longer.

Get out!
And don't come back!

So we'll lose our shot
at the commission.
I'll find another way.
A better path.
I curse myself
for ever thinking
this man could be my chance.

He studies me.
I wait, wonder

if he'll strike.
But when his arm darts out,
it's not at me. He yanks my canvas
from the easel.

My heart is in my throat.
Susanna.

Start over.
This time with some
perspective.

He wrenches the canvas
from the bars it's stretched upon.
He pins me with his gaze
while calloused hands
rend my heart
like it's nothing.
Like I'm nothing.

And then Susanna's lying on the floor in
shreds.

48.

Susanna did not let
those monsters
maul her and I can't leave
the pieces of her story
on the floor.

But as I gather shredded canvas,
hold her to my breast,
I see a righteous woman,
pure and virtuous.

She was all that.

She also fought her parents tooth and
    nail
when they betrothed her to Joaquim.
(This isn't in the scriptures
but my mother told me so.)

I can't quite grasp
why she would fight

against the chance to leave
her parents' house.
There can be no worse captor than my
    father.
Even a man

    who drinks and
    shouts and
    shoves

would get me out.

Mother never told me tales
of girls
who settled
for the least
appalling option.

But Mother isn't here now.

Don't be hasty.

But until Susanna's been used to grind
    pigments

and stretch canvas when she has more
  talent
than he could ever dream of . . .

It's so dangerous.
Be careful.

But she stayed behind a wall
and still they found her.
I'm done being careful.

197

Tame

Careful, love. If we're not quiet, we'll wake the boys. And then I won't be able to tell you what happens next for Judith. Because this story is only for you. The boys have all the tales they need of brave warriors and army captains.

It takes Judith and Abra surprisingly little effort to get past the captain's guard — a lifted skirt, a saucy smile, a promise to deliver exactly what the captain needs. With nothing more, the women pass inside the tent.

When their eyes adjust, they make out the captain hunched over maps and battle plans. He barely registers their presence. But Judith will wait as long as it takes, Abra at her side.

(This shows you her determination,

love, for Judith is no more patient than you are.)

Finally the captain grunts, pushes back from his maps, and glances into the darkness. "Don't just stand there. I haven't got much time."

Judith steps forward, into the circle of light cast by his lamp.

He drinks her in, mistakes the blaze in her eyes for something else entirely. "Then again, I was just about to take my supper. Please sit down." He shouts toward the outside of the tent, "Bring this young lady some wine."

"No, sir. Thank you. I have brought my own provisions. I mean not to inconvenience you in any way."

A slow smile melts across his face, where a scar runs from his right ear, across his cheek to his upper lip. Judith lingers on what sort of blade made that cut, how much force it took. She allows herself the fleeting fantasy that Malachi reached this very spot, left that mark, and now she's here to finish what he started.

It barely matters if it's true. The thought's enough to still her shaking knees.

"I don't think that will be a problem." The captain's eyes flicker to Abra. "Your girl can wait outside."

Judith feels Abra's hesitation, but this is not the time to be more sister than servant. One sharp glance at Abra and Judith is alone with the captain of the Assyrian army. How many soldiers before her tried to get here? How many failed at the end of his sword?

But Malachi's here too, and that will get Judith through whatever's coming.

"I think you should know," she begins, then falters. Judith summons her courage. It's a gamble to show her hand but something tells her this man will enjoy the game more if she does. "I am a woman of the Hebrews."

The captain startles, recovers quickly. "It will be a shame to have to kill you."

Judith paints on a mask of cunning. She bats her eyelashes, curls her lips in girlish coquetry. The words she must say are hardly pillow talk, but if she plays it right, they just might have the same effect. "I've fled from them to you, to show you how to get through the mountains without the loss of a single soldier."

The captain pays attention to her words. He also pays attention to her neckline. "And why would you do that?"

Now is the time to spread before him a banquet he will not refuse. (He could, but he will choose not to.) "I have heard of your wisdom, your policies, and your excellence is reported in all the earth, that you are mighty in knowledge and wonderful in feats of war."

Judith has drawn close enough to straddle him. He is a beast to tame before the slaughter. There's something twisted about doing this for love, but this is war and everything is twisted.

She lowers herself onto his lap, steadies her breath as his rough hands slide up her legs.

"Your words are as beautiful as your form."

Bile rises in Judith's throat.

"If you please, sir" — his breath is hot upon her neck — "my people have turned from the one true God" — his fingers travel up her back — "and He has sent me here to work with you as your servant" —

in her hair, on her throat — "and together what we accomplish will astonish all the earth."

A deep growl rumbles through the beast. "My servant?"

No turning back now. "Ready and willing."

And then he devours her.

49.

Judith is not careful,
no pure and virtuous woman.
She would not let a man
shove her down,
banish her from the studio
only to call her back again
to be a prop.

It's not that I've abandoned
Susanna

      (I couldn't)

but more than that:
      a thrumming surges
      through my veins
      since Tino showed his hand.

Something fiery,
fierce, impassioned.
Echoes of Judith,

widow of Bethulia.
My mother's Judith.
As with Susanna,
the men get her wrong.

Father's Judith cradles
a pristine severed head
like the baby she never knew
she longed for.

Allori's porcelain-faced warrior
wears not a speck of blood
as she displays the captain's head
like a basket of fresh-cut flowers.

Caravaggio's Judith shows
vague concern as she glides
her blade through a tender cut of
meat.

The men do not paint the blood.
But blood's the heart of Judith.
My mother did not hold back
on the blood when she told me
Judith's truth.

How can anyone capture her
without understanding
the horror of her actions,
the strength it took,
the stains that stayed forever?

How does the body's life force
leave its vessel while
the heart still beats
but the end has begun?

I'm only guessing —
I'm no da Vinci
yet I know the heart is powerful
and so the blood must arc
in great, triumphal bursts.
It must splatter Judith's breast,
          her servant's face.

This is no moment of passion.
This is war.

I paint the blood.

Consider

What's coming next is not the stuff of bedtime stories. It may frighten you. It should.

When Judith's back hits the pallet, even she wonders if she can do this. She cannot change her course, but still she considers: might it be better to turn the sword on herself? Or worse, join his side? Forget her husband's sacrifice, her people, her faithful servant, and stay in the suffocating embrace of this monster?

Because he is a monster. But he's strong, and powerful, and from most perspectives, he's on the winning side. She has to ask herself — and women have asked themselves this question for centuries — would she rather be suffocated slowly for the rest of her life, or die

quickly trying to accomplish something?
(What would you choose, love?)
There will be no more asking questions
once a sword is in her hand.

50.

Tuzia appears,
a grizzled apparition
of my future
as a maidservant to men.

She doesn't usually climb the stairs,
just hollers from below
because her hips
     her knees
     her aching feet betray her.

But now she scowls
from the doorway
at my canvas
covered in triumphal
arcs of blood.

She is no artist,
but this art pays her wages.
We share a bedroom,
endure the men together.

Is it so much to wish
the only other woman
in this house
might see my work
and understand?

Apparently it is.

What is it, Tuzia?

Anyway it's all
first fire now.
How could she
make meaning
from a canvas
filled with blood?

> *I have not seen Signor Tassi
> in days.*

Her girlish crush
grates on me,
pestle on mortar.

I shouldn't judge.
She's not the first
to be swayed
by Tino's wink,
his smile.

That's none of my concern.

Is he not your teacher?

Not anymore.

I turn back to Judith,
turn back to the blood.

Wonder

Judith must distract herself from the task at hand (and neck and breast and calf). Instead of the pressing, weighty, smothering things at the forefront of her mind, Judith prepares for the blood.

Driving a sword through a man's neck is bound to be messy, after all.

(It is not my place to tell your father how to paint. But have you ever noticed how little blood his Judiths have?)

Though she prepares herself, even Judith has no idea how much blood there will be. Whether it will dribble out, tepid, or erupt, scorching, with so much force it splatters her breasts, her mouth, her eyes, intermingles with her fear, her rage, her gut instinct to protect her people, avenge her husband, and make sense of what she's lost.

However much blood there will be, Judith is certain the captain pinning her down at this very moment is a powerfully strong man. His whole being will spring into action the moment he feels a blade against his neck.

She thinks his muscled arms will flail up in the faces of two women bearing down on him with all their might. For soon it will be her turn.

Soon she will be on top.

51.

The hours float by
on a torrent of blood.
I don't know how long
I paint; I only know
my hands are covered
in vermillion.
My face is streaked as well.

When boots clomp up the stairs
I brace for complaints:
> I'm wasting time
> on Judith's blood
> instead of doing a client's bidding.
But Judith took off a head.
I can handle Father.

Instead:

Getting messy?

Sudden havoc

in my heart,
fumbling panic.
I shove my skirts down,
streak my legs with red,
and grope for Judith,
as though some paint on canvas
could guide me,
shield me,
tell me why
he'd return
after what he broke the last time.

I told you not to come back.

I try to force the trembling
from my voice.

> *Watch your passion.*
> *It's dangerous.*

What can he tell a woman
about danger?

He studies my canvas.
I hate his eyes on Judith.

You've done worse.

I no longer care about pleasing you.

Except I do.
If he changed his tune,
took me on for the Quirinal,
told me again I am the painter
in this house,
I would find a way
to forget.

But what does that make me?

It's such a pity your father
can't see your progress.
Does that bother you?

There's no cajoling now.
No soothing words

and promises.
I turned him down.

Such sins cannot be forgiven.

Of course, I have only
to tell him you're
        progressing
and he'll be even more
        besotted
with me than before.

He's a worthless talent, your
        father,
but as friends go, he's
        incredibly loyal.
He'd never deny me a thing
        I asked for.

I am not a thing,
to be handed
from one man
to another.

He advances on my easel
but I will not let him
touch my work again.

> *You forget your place, little*
> *girl.*

You don't scare me.

> *I'm still owed*
> *payment for your lessons.*

I'll be sure you're paid in full.

> *You certainly will.*

Something has shifted,
a glint in his eye,
a thing that makes him monstrous
but could flip around
and charm a queen.

We're done here.

I cringe at the youth
— the fear —
in my voice.
I've no authority.
He is teacher, I am student,
man and girl
power, nothing.

We're done painting.

His fingers dig into
my arm.
The sudden realization
of what's going to happen next

descends

a weight upon
my chest
impossible to dodge.
I focus on those pulsing points of pain,
his fingers digging in.
It's going to grow so much worse

but if I keep my focus

on one constant bit of
suffering

I might survive.

Survive

Judith survives.

Remember this, my love, if nothing else: Judith survives what should destroy her.

She gasps for breath beneath the captain's arm — a fallen tree across her body would weigh less. His breath reeks of wine and meat and man. She tolerated it before, but now he's passed out, drunk on more than wine. For how long, though, there's no time to stop and wonder.

He mutters something as Judith wrestles from beneath his heft. She freezes until he's still again. Then Judith sits, pulls on her dress, and tries to force from her mind the ache between her legs, the echo of his grunts, the smell, the taste, the choking fear.

(I do not tell you these things to frighten you. You will not know for many years, my love, but it is not always like that. I promise.)

For Judith, there will be time later to remember, and hopefully forget. Right now, though, she must focus.

She fetches Abra — faithful Abra — hunched outside, a captive audience to every grunt and heave. Abra edges inside the tent, face white, eyes skating from her lady's hair and rumpled dress to the passed-out monster mere feet away.

"We have to do this," Judith says.

Abra doesn't move.

"Now."

Abra's voice is barely more than a breath. "You're sure he won't wake up?"

Of course he'll wake up. Beheadings are nasty that way. Judith knows this. It's why she must be sure the moment he awakes, the blade is halfway through the neck.

"You know the plan."

Abra's breath comes in short gasps.

Judith grasps her servant, her sister, by the hands.

"Abra. I need you more than ever. So breathe and prepare yourself. We're already in motion."

Abra's hands stir inside Judith's. She squeezes back. She isn't sure, but she will move forth anyway, because her sister told her to.

(Sometimes that's all you need, my love — another woman's faith in you.)

As they made their way to the camp, Judith repeated the plan more times than Abra has fetched water from a well: On the count of three, Abra will press down on the captain's chest with all her strength. She'll kneel on him if she has to. Judith will be ready with the sword, moving fast enough so his throat's cut before he can scream.

Judith hauls the captain's sword from the side of his pallet, where he kept it at the ready even after he'd stripped off all else. She staggers under its weight. If she can barely lift the sword, how can she possibly carry out this deed?

Abra waits for her command. Judith is the captain now.

"Be ready for blood," she murmurs.

"Blood?"

"One . . ."

"Judith!"

"Two . . ."

"I don't —"

"Three!"

52.

At five or six years old,
my only knowledge of the studio
was the fumes wafting down the stairs.
But overcome with curiosity,
I snuck inside one day, surveyed
the beckoning pots of paint.

I started slapping color
on the canvas.
I didn't understand
what Father knew:
everything that came before
was as important as,
more important than
the act of painting.

Without stretching
and greasing the canvas,
straining the oil through linen,
extracting the impurities
and grinding the colors,

there was no painting.

I barely remember my father's rage
when he laid eyes on the canvas I
    ruined.
What's forever entrenched:
the stab to my gut when the colors,
so glorious in my mind,
globbed together,
dribbled down,
puddled on the floor
like a child's accident.
Because sometimes
it doesn't turn out
the way you thought it would.
Sometimes what you imagine
in your head isn't what comes out
of the paintbrush.

And then you start to realize
something has gone horribly, horribly
    wrong,
and there'll never be a way to put it back
    the way it was.

Escape

The deed is done. You might think the story ends here. In some versions, it does. But Judith is nowhere near safe. Perhaps that's why she can't release the captain's sword.

Blood still gushes from his neck, while the head lolls on the ground. The thud it made on impact reverberates in Judith's brain. She's slick with residue. There's no time to wash away the terror.

Someone will have heard the struggle. They would have expected to hear a struggle of some sort. But now it's quiet. Soldiers can smell blood. They could burst in at any moment. Still, Judith cannot unclamp her fingers from the weapon.

"Judith. We have to go."

Abra's voice jolts Judith from whatever spell has clutched her in its grip. She scrambles off the body, horror-stricken that she stayed astride a moment longer than she had to.

Clear, tangible actions. These will save Judith. Or at least give her the best chance. "We have to take the head."

Abra stumbles to the far corner of the tent. "I'm not touching it."

"You don't have to." Judith crosses to the head, forces herself to look directly at what she's done.

"Don't you want his soldiers to see it?"

"I'd love for his soldiers to see it. To see the terror on the great warrior's face. But spite serves no one and our people will need the assurance he's dead. Get me the basket of bread."

Abra stares at Judith as though she's just suggested they stop and have a bite to eat.

Voices in the distance — but not distant enough — finally loosen Judith's fingers from the sword. She scrambles for the basket of provisions and the head.

No time for revulsion. No time for va-

227

cant eyes that showed no life even before the throat was slit, or dangling bits of sinew, dripping blood.

Judith hoists the head, heavier than expected, into the basket. She covers it, as though that will block out the horror. Her plan only went this far. But there is so much farther still to go.

53.

Blood stains
        my hands
    my dress.

Mingled with the blood,
        paint.

   Which is which,
I do not know,
      which is me
      (maybe both),
only that I will never be
          pure
    again.

    Part of me longs

to crawl behind an easel,
    curl up in a ball,

sleep forever.

But also power surges
through my veins,

I long to run
as hard and fast as I can
until my feet bleed —

why is there

so much
blood?

I'm torn between the urges,
curl up   or sprint
and somehow instead of
either
I stand and stare
at the blood
on my hands.

When I paint
I spend more time

on hands than faces.

Anyone can paint a face —
two eyes, a mouth, a nose.

Hands are so much more
complex,
tell whole stories of their own:
clenched fists, ecstatic palms,
fearful fingers white with
terror.

Mine are no longer white.

54.

I'm staring at my hands, still,
　　　hours later,
　　　　　maybe days.

The planet's stopped
or whirls around too fast
to grab on to a branch,
a hand, an anchor
that will keep me
tethered to this world.
And then:

　　　　There's a choice to be made.

Judith stands beside me.
not an

　　　　image on my canvas
　　　　voice in my head
　　　　story of my mother's

but so real she's cradling
my bloody hand in hers.

*Right now, in this instant
you have to make a choice.*

I open my mouth to speak —
the first words I've uttered
since I screamed, *Let me go!*

(I think I screamed.
I'm almost sure
I tried to fight.
Those minutes pierce my brain
with brutal clarity
while also blurring
at the edges.)

*This was supposed to be
the beginning.*

It still is.

Susanna.
She's pristine as ever,
Judith's opposite
but just as real.
She extends a hand
but I don't want to stain
her lovely robes
        perfect skin
        untarnished soul.

She did not let them touch her.

I cannot meet Susanna's eye
or Judith's.
Instead my gaze falls
        on streaks of red
    everywhere I look.

My dress.

            Not just your dress.

Susanna sits next to me

on the floor,
holds out her hand again.
When did I sit?

Easels loom over me,
                    monsters, cages.
Easels where I've passed my life —
for what?

Is this all I get?

Susanna says nothing.
Just places her hand
on mine.

All my work.
All my talent . . .

Judith's voice
is a sword
at my throat.

                    Right now?

This is all you get.

I wrench my hands away
      — hands tell whole stories of their
      own —
and stumble to my feet.

Pain knifes through me
but it's barely a drop
      in the deluge of horror.

I have to get out.
I can't be here now.
I can still feel him —

Judith stands before the window,
blocks my flight.

      You'll always feel him.
      There's nowhere to go.

If that's true,
    if there's nowhere to go,
there's nothing left but to feel the wave,

to let it wash over me,
   drown me,
         drag me under,
fill my lungs.

Come to us.
Come to us.

55.

i've got a secret for you

        shut out the rest

      echoes of the tales
my mother used to tell
        her force of will
the missing color

      if there are impurities
        the painting will be ruined
but this is now not then

what else matters
i'm only back where i started

      two things colliding
vanishing points

no idea
how much blood there
would be
it means they like you

hands covered with paint
but i would know

echoes of the tales
my mother used to tell
if i burn my hands

we're done painting

i'll tell you another secret

right this very moment
i can play the part
it would be over quickly

if i wait it out
i might survive
just pigment on canvas

(portrait of
a little girl)

    a sudden knowledge
like the point
on the horizon
      once they've gotten
        what they asked for

    her force of will
the missing color

but this isn't about strength
          it no longer matters
nothing that can be
described with words
just an image i can't
righteous
impurities
    blood, water, paint

the line is only perceived
a trick of the eye
                    potentially world-altering

but then
you never see the beast
until he is upon you

        echoes of the tales
my mother used to tell
            her force of will
the missing color

PART IV

Sinful

Not all stories have happy endings. I cannot promise this one will either. But I am certain you will be glad you stayed with Susanna to the end. She deserves that much — a witness, one who says I see you, hear you, I'm better for knowing your story.

Right now, it is Rebecca's story too. She shrieks, hysterical, undone. Susanna's sister has lost all thought for decency. (And decency, my love, is sometimes better shed.) Her petty jealousies have fallen away in the face of such injustice. Her beautiful younger sister, purity itself, stands bound, surrounded, streaked with dirt. Rebecca is, herself, tearstained, aflame with fury. She tears at her hair as the village looks on. She's never cared less what people thought of her.

Any moment stones will fly.

This is no metaphor. On the word of those two elders at the wall, Susanna is set to be stoned as a faithless wife. If Joaquim were here, he might believe her, stand for her. But without him, it is only the word of a woman against the word of two men.

Rebecca shrieks at her sister to speak. She shrieks at the crowd to show compassion, to listen. Her sister is no sinner! They know this!

But when Susanna finally speaks, her words are not what Rebecca would have her say.

"Would you like a list of my sins before you hurl those rocks at my head?"

Rebecca cannot understand why her sister would give the crowd further ammunition. Why she would ever concede a single fault. A woman accused has no room for fault.

"She is righteous!" Rebecca cries to the crowd. "She is raving and terrified, but she is righteous!"

"I am a sinner." Susanna's voice is

steady, carrying throughout the crowd, amplified by the energy of their judgment. "I am prideful. I wear my righteousness like a shield. I feign ignorance of beggars in the street. I push away my own loving sister. I lie — but not about this.

"And now? Now I harbor hatred. Now I long to grab a rock of my own and hurl it at those who would unjustly accuse me when they are the sinners and I did nothing more than attempt to bathe in my private garden.

"These are my sins."

Except there is one more: Susanna is a woman.

56.

Brush in hand,
I do not move.

I used to know
what it was for
but now I can't
connect this thing
to any purpose.

57.

Wakefulness slices
through my sleep
like a shaft of light
from Caravaggio's own brush.
I'm seized with the need
to rid my dress of the stain
it still bears.

I stumble from bed
without a care for who might hear;
I know now no one will come.
I drag behind me what I wore
that day, which Tuzia washed
and returned, rust-brown streaks and
    all.
I do not own a single garment
unblemished by my craft.
What's the difference, she must think.

It's oil and water
and all the impurities

settle at the
bottom.

I could discard it, burn it.
But I will not allow him
one more thing of mine.
As small as it might seem

    a worthless dress

in this moment
nothing has ever mattered more.
If Tuzia cannot remove the stain
      if my father cannot keep monsters
        from my home
        if my brothers will not come
          when I scream

then I will do it for
my self.

I shove the stained cloth against
the ridges of the washboard
with so much force

my hand
will be sore tomorrow.
It doesn't matter;
it's not like I can paint.
What good are hands?

Despite the blooming ache in my fingers
the familiarity of the task
soothes the ragged edge inside.
I kneel here every month.

Tuzia does my washing,
except for when I bleed.
     (You'd think she never bled
     the way she turns her nose up,
     acts as though I've soiled myself.)

If she were to rouse herself from sleep
and see me now
she'd just assume
I fight against
the stain of womanhood.

But — oh God —
oh Holy Mother —

I have not bled
in many weeks.
I choke on a sob of realization.

> *There now,*
> *you can't be sure.*

Susanna kneels beside me.

Judith takes over my labors
at the washboard.

> *You'll know soon enough.*

I cannot —

> *Of course not.*

> *But there are other ways . . .*

Ways to die.

Ways to bear
the eternal guilt
of mortal sin.

Ways to line the pockets
of herbwives claiming
to hold the cure
for unwanted lives, coercion, regrets.

I'll never be rid of him.

And never have I
wanted more to bleed.

58.

The night my mother
finally slipped
from pain
                    to nothingness
I slumped to sleep
with tear-drenched sheets
and woke to blood.

      Streaks of muddy red
      on dingy gray —
          the remnants on a palette after
          painting battlefields.

I was no soldier, only girl
without a mother
or the sense to understand
this world without her.

I groped
without a mother
to find a source

for the blood
but the only wound was
my severed heart.

Perhaps the wreckage
had seeped through
my pores, my tears, my sweat
to stain the sheets.
Without a mother,
I thought at first
     I'm dying too.

     (I was. I am.
     But this expiration
     will linger and stretch,
     meander across the
     months and years
     until there's nothing left
     of me to drain.)

Any other day
     — a day that still contained my
       mother —
I would have realized sooner

what I finally came to know
without a mother:
I bled as she did
with the moon,
not illness or infirmity.

On that morning, though,
I was addled
by exhaustion
and grief
and so instead
I wept myself to sleep
again amidst the blood.

Without a mother.

59.

I sleep-walked
through the first few
motherless days,
a trail of blood reminding me
I'd have no guide
through marriage
childbirth
womanhood.

When Father called me to the studio
I climbed the stairs in certainty
he meant to send me to the home
for inconvenient girls.
Enclosed within the convent
he'd be spared the shadow of
his wife's
cheekbones, heavy jaw,
defiant gaze at every turn.

He swore at the canvas
as I reached the top

(how was he painting then,
my mother barely cold,
the sister that she bore
an echo of the life she might have
   lived?)

and beckoned me forward
without a glance.

Fetch me a palette knife,

I did not know a palette knife
from kitchen knife, not then.

Right there!
The flat, round blade!

I held it out, an offering.
He clutched my hand
for just a moment
as he took the knife.

Prudentia . . .

258

My heart stood still.
I thought it might be better
to betroth myself to Christ
than stay, remind my father
what he'd lost.
Remind us both.

He cleared his throat.

Burnt umber.

Father?

*I need more pigment
ground!
Can you manage that or
not?*

I could.

And so I was betrothed
to art instead.

60.

I am a wife
unable to fulfill
her duties.

Every day I sit
before the canvas
hoping maybe
hand or heart
will make the leap.

And so I'm sitting, staring,
when I hear a clomp upon the stairs.
Father will nag —
        why am I not doing
        the work that pays the bills?

Instead:

        New technique?

I scramble off the stool

fly across the studio,
as far as I can get
from Agostino.

His voice
His breath
His breadth
are always in my thoughts
      but why
      is he here
      in the flesh?

He should be covered in my blood.

Get out.

He smiles, as though
we're lovers, and
I've made a little joke.

                Don't be mean.

Tuzia is down below.

If I call out,
she'll come.

Won't she?

> *What's wrong, darling?*
> *Is it your father again?*

He reaches out a hand
but pauses
when I flinch.

> *You know I'll never*
> *let anything happen to*
> *   you.*
> *I snuck out of the palace*
> *as soon as I could.*
> *I've been buried in work.*
> *Are you angry?*
> *You know I never*
> *stop thinking of*
> *my Artemisia.*

61.

I told him no
I said stop
I screamed
I clawed

I know I did —

*I never stop
thinking of
my Artemisia.*

— I think

But now he speaks as though
we shared ourselves,
the only blood the product
of our pounding hearts —

That's not right.

Susanna's gentle voice

insists I listen.

You know who you are.
You know your truth.

I take
Susanna's hand.

My darling —

— No.
I am done thinking of you.
And you are not welcome
in my studio.

He chuckles.

It is my studio.

You're the master,
*   are you?*
At seventeen years
*   of age?*

I understand perspective.
And that's all you had to offer.

He settles onto
my stool, familiar,
leans forward, earnest,
my confidant.
He rearranges
my brushes.

> *My darling girl.*
> *Why are you so*
> > *determined*
>
> *to push me away?*

> *Your father believes*
> *your lessons should*
> > *continue —*

My father is a blind fool
who wants to keep me
a student and a child,
and I'm no longer either.

His gaze skates over my dress.

> *You're not a child.*

My stomach roils.
I hold fast
to the anchor
of Susanna's hand
in my own.

He's actually impressed by you,
by your second-rate frescoes,
your filthy mouth.
He'll see what you are,
but by the time he does,
I'll be so far gone
neither one of you
will ever reach me.

> *You're ambitious,*
>   *Artemisia.*
> *But without me?*
> *You'll never fulfill*
> *your potential.*

His eyes land on a sketch
from before my hands stopped
    moving —
another version of Susanna,
one where she stands
and looks the monsters in the eye.

He reaches for the sketch.
He'll rip it like he did before.

I lunge, snatch Susanna,
send Agostino toppling
off the stool
before I scramble down the stairs.

Arrive

They run as though they will be torn limb from limb if they are caught. And they will.

Mile upon mile, stumbling over rocky terrain in the dark, panicking at every crack of a branch, every animal call. Judith wrestles with the heavy basket, her arms aching, the adrenaline exhausted miles ago. Abra wrestles with her terror. Her body is strong from a lifetime of hauling water and children and waste, but she is no soldier.

And this is war.

Finally they reach the gates. Abra lunges for the rope to ring the bell that brings the watchmen in the night. But Judith uses the last of her strength to stay Abra's arm.

"Wait," she gasps.

Abra's lost all respect for station. "I didn't run all this way to sit as prey outside my own city gates."

"Only for a moment, Abra." Judith's legs shake beneath her, but if she sinks to the ground now, she may never stand again. She sets the basket down, turns away from it. "I have to think of what to say. Everyone will come when they hear the gates opening at night. They won't believe we've done this on our own, not to mention that little matter of a large man's head in a basket!"

Abra gives Judith her moment. But no more than that. In a single day she has gone from a life of drudgery, every day the same, scrubbing, cooking, hauling, to breaking into an enemy camp, aiding in the seduction of the captain, then helping to take off his head.

A snort of amusement escapes and Abra claps a hand over her mouth. But then a full-blown chuckle grows beyond the point where she can control it. Judith stares in horror.

"I'm sorry," Abra gasps. "But this whole

thing is funny, if you think about it. You don't hesitate to slice off a man's head, but you're shaking at the prospect of knocking on your home city's gates."

Suddenly Judith sees the humor too — the utterly horrifying humor.

"You don't think I hesitated?" she says, deadly serious, and yet she cannot stop her own hysterical giggle. "You don't think it was the most horrible, gruesome thing I've ever done in my entire life?"

Abra's laughter dies in her throat. "I only went along with you because you were so sure!"

Judith would never show uncertainty to a servant. But after sharing this night with her, Abra would never be her servant again. "I wasn't sure of anything."

"Then what were we doing there?"

"What no one else could." The laughter has passed. Judith retrieves the basket. "Ring the bell."

62.

The stairs do not descend
into some unknown depths,
do not deliver me
to another life
where I might still have
a chance as artist, bride.

I face only
the same four walls
as every other day.
I make it almost
to the door
when boots
come clomping
down behind me.

If Tino should chase me
through the streets
I'd be the one
to look the fool
or worse.

I duck into
our tiny pantry,
inhale onions, garlic,
rot.

Two men who hold
my future
in their hands
stand feet away
from where I —

> . . . *insolent girl,*
> *lazy and prone to*
> *flights of fancy.*

— gasp for breath.

The front door slams
and slams again
as Father hurries after
Agostino, to beg
forgiveness from
my rapist.

63.

The stool.

I want it to burn
now that Tino's
marred it with
his touch.

The brushes.
The easel.
The dress.

He's touched everything.
I'd have to burn myself to ash
before his touch could be erased.

But when I turn one way
I see the wreckage of Susanna:
                she did not yield.
The other way is Judith,
straining to lift a sword
she never asked for.

They could have both been killed.

Susanna would have been
if not for Daniel, who lent
his voice and saved her life.

(Imagine that: a man who stands
up for a woman's truth.)

       Not Daniel's voice.

Susanna,
always there,
unafraid to speak.

       My own voice saved me.
       Use your voice.

I can barely
find my footing,
much less . . .

       Much less lift a brush?

Judith,
not so soft,
(and how could she be
to do what she did?)

Much less survive.

Judith turns to me, points to
my paintbrush.

I need you.

I don't have a sword.

She reaches out,
her hands bloodstained,
and wraps my fingers
around the brush.

> *They paint me*
> *nubile and dainty and weak.*
> *They make a beheading*
> *look like an orgasm.*

It was bloody.

> *You have no idea.*
> *Or maybe you do.*

It was bloody.

It was bloody.

> *Why are women expected*
> *to be afraid of blood?*

Susanna.

> *We spend half our lives*
> *cleaning it up.*

> *It runs through our veins,*
> *spills from the source.*

> *Paint the blood.*
> *Paint the blood.*

I don't want to.

I know.
We know.

64.

Before I can paint the blood
it's creeping down my thigh,
both razor-sharp reminder
and relief so deep
I'm on my knees
to the patron saint
of women who do not wish
to pass along their wounds
to one who may be innocent
but still would bring to mind
with every breath and kick and heartbeat
how much different life would be
if they had never been conceived.

65.

This time
when the front door creaks
and Tuzia's girlish laughter
drifts up the stairs
I'm ready.

Perspective was never
Tino's to teach me.
I know this now.

Familiar boots on the stairs.

A shadow in the door frame.

You are not small.

Judith reminds me.

I am not small.
I am painting the blood.
I keep my voice steady

even though
my hands shake.
I speak before he can,
as though his answer
doesn't even matter.

Leave. Now.

> *You're not nearly*
> *as hospitable as*
> *they say you are.*

I want to let his words
fly out the open window,
dust that settles
on the stones below
and turns to mud
in the rain. But still
I flinch.

> *Oh, my Artemisia.*
> *We used to laugh*
> *   together.*
> *Those fools who think*

they know you —
it matters not what they
say.

It's you and I
against the world.
Always has been.
Nothing's changed.

The first time,
he made me small.
The last time
I panicked, fled.
This time I look to Judith.
Just beyond my easel,
her eyes bore into mine.
This time I'll stand
my ground.

Everything has changed.
I'm going to tell my father.

Judith nods.

But Tino acts as though
I haven't spoken,
he hasn't understood,
doesn't care.
He wanders through the studio,
laying casual claim
to all he sees.

I'm going to tell my father.
What you did to me.

He pauses,
doesn't turn around.
It's not that I want
him to look at me
      speak to me,
I only want
him to acknowledge
I have a voice
and things to say.

          What did I
          do to you?

He cannot make me
       say it
       live it.
Words have power.
He won't take mine again.

You think you've gotten away
with this but you haven't.

                I still don't follow.

He lounges by the window,
disturbs a pair of mourning doves
nestled on the sill,
crushes a honeysuckle tendril
that dared curl its way inside.
Anybody walking by
could spy him
inside my studio.
My father's studio.

But that's the point.

What was wrong,
with taking what you
    offered?

You have weapons.

Judith is Abra at my side.

You're not defenseless this time.

Offering is not
how I'll describe
it to the judge.

    The judge!
    Your imagination
        astounds —
    that's your artist's heart
        at play.
    Your strength,
    till it's your weakness.

    But here are the facts,
        my love:

our laws
do not allow a little girl
to bring a charge of any
  sort
before the court.
In short: even if what you
  said
were true, you can't do
  anything to me.

A brush, a palette knife,
a stool, a bit of canvas.
A daughter.
If he should be charged
with anything,
it won't be attacking me.
It will be damaging
my father's property.

Still.

My father can.

Your father!

*Your father, who invited
me here?*

*Who has always been
right downstairs?*

*In this fantasy you're
spinning,*

I've deflowered you

*and left your heart in
ruins, yes?*

If Judith had a sword
to wield this moment
I'd never get the blood
off my walls.
I am the one
who takes her trembling hand.
I know what's coming,
feel it like the moments before
a fat, dark rain cloud
opens up and drowns
a mouse in the gutter.

*Your father will be utterly
unsurprised*

by news that you're a
whore.

You've damaged his property.
He won't take kindly to that.

> *You were damaged*
> *goods*
> *long before I touched*
> *you.*
> *That's what I'll say,*
> *if anyone should ask.*

> *Or perhaps*
> *even if they don't.*

287

66.

A spider treks across the studio,
his route the stretch of ground
beside my face.
Someone should sweep.
It won't be me.

Breathing is a chore.

From my chosen perspective,
            Father is a monster.
He looms above,
muttering obscenities;
the angle magnifies
his bulk,
his rage.

But that's the thing about perspective.
The slightest shift
transforms the subject.

If I should shift

and look him in the eye,
I cannot say what I would see.
Not monster, though, I think.
More like beast
who lashes out in fear.

Atop my stool,
he grumbles at his own attempts
to compose a decent Lucretia.

> The focal point
> of Father's version
> is not the agony
> she must feel
> moments before
> she ends her life,
> but rather the breast
> into which she will plunge
> her dagger.

If I'd found Father
stumbling over

the female form
a month ago, I would have pitied
him and fixed the faults
when he went out to drink.

But now I cannot paint.

Father does not understand
what's changed. Suddenly his secret
weapon's blade has dulled.
His paintings do not magically
improve at night.
He has to do the work
he signs his name upon
while I lie useless
on the ground.

I'm only in the studio
because there's nowhere else to go.

67.

That's not quite true.

I am also here
because the studio
is where I tell
my truth.

If I can find the strength.

You will.

But Susanna only knows her story.
Not mine.

Father flings the paintbrush down.
It lands next to my head,
splatters on my cheek.
I do not wipe it off.

He grunts and stomps across the floor.
I do not ask —

he'll tell me soon enough.

And here it is:

> *We've taken on more work*
> *than I can handle on my*
> *own!*

I sigh.
He's never understood
Susanna's terror.
How could he begin
to understand mine?
I start with something simple.
(Nothing's simple.)

I will take no further lessons
from Signor Tassi.

My father laughs.

> *You will not do the work*
> *required*
> *to keep us from the streets*

and yet you'll also kill my
only chance
at his commission?

I have learned perspective.
What do my lessons —

> *Don't play the fool, girl.*
> *He likes you.*
> *A far sight more than he*
> *likes me.*
> *And if his infatuation*
> *can make this family's*
> *fortune —*

He raped me.

68.

I've choked on truth
for so many weeks
and now it's finally out
I'm outraged
Father didn't know.

How could he see me day to day

     ghostly pale,
     not from enclosure in the studio
     but from the strain
     of anything beyond
     survival

     stuttered breaths,
     erratic, jagged
     shards of pottery
     smashed on the floor

     hands that refuse
     to grasp

a brush

and not put the broken pieces
together?

I won't let him
avert his eyes
any longer.

> *You need to think very*
> *carefully*
> *before you utter another*
> *word —*

He raped me.

> *A lover's quarrel —*

He raped me!

My shriek echoes
off the walls of my cell.
My brothers must have heard
and Tuzia.

But then they may have heard
the rape itself.
No one came running then
and still they do not come.

69.

Maybe my brothers were too busy
at their studies to hear my screams,
memorizing ancient texts,
the stories passed
from men
to boys.

Maybe Francesco couldn't answer,
too busy reciting
his Ovid.
Perhaps *Lucretia,* like yesterday
while I was chopping onions
for his supper.

> *"Three times she tried to speak,*
> *three times desisted,*
> *And a fourth time, gaining courage,*
> *still couldn't raise her eyes.*
> *She said: 'Must I owe this to a*
> *Tarquin too? Must I speak,*
> *Speak, poor wretch, my shame*

from my own mouth?' "

I may not know how to read,
but I know how to overhear
the stories men
tell boys
of women's lives.

> *"What she could, she told. The end
>   she suppressed.*
> *She wept, and a blush spread over
>   a wife's cheeks.*
> *Her husband and her father forgave
>   her being forced:*
> *she said: 'I deny myself the
>   forgiveness that you grant.'*
> *Then she stabbed herself with a
>   blade she had hidden,*
> *And, all bloodied, fell at her father's
>   feet."*

Mother whispered our stories
in my ear.

*"Even then she took care in dying
so that she fell
With decency, that was her care
even in falling."*

The men and boys shout
theirs at full volume.

70.

I am not sure you understand.
If you go spreading this nonsense —

Nonsense!

You are the one who will suffer,
not Agostino.

He is not wrong, and yet.

If you had a sword,
you wouldn't turn it on yourself.

I am already suffering.
And your property has been damaged.

He sets the palette down.

I did not send you away
upon your mother's death
or any day since then.
We will cry foul on my
*   property*
if necessary but
do not act as though
you are a brush I've used
and thrown away once you
*   were worn.*

Then help me!

All of the blame,
all of the accusations
will be yours to bear.
Even if you are to be
*   believed*
you are the one who will no
*   longer*
be able to show her face.
No society.
No marriage.

I only meant to say the words.

> *What's more, if this defines*
> *you,*
> *there will be no painting.*

This should not shock me.
And yet I feel it like a blade
upon my skin.

And without me to paint
how ever will you survive
the Roman art world?

> *That is hardly my concern.*

That's your only concern!

> *If you say this —*

I've already said it.

> *Outside these walls?*

Only the slimmest
remaining shred
of concern for decency
keeps me from lunging
for the open window,
screaming into the narrow alley,
to echo off the paving stones,
be carried by the creeping ivy
into every home.

No.

            But you mean to. You are
                  decided.

I weigh my next words carefully.

He put a brush into my hands
but never quill and parchment,
never books.
Words and paragraphs
were gifts bestowed upon my brothers.
But my mother gave me stories.
The ones she chose to tell

were not an accident,
not fevered ramblings
but the sharpest blade
that she could leave me on her death.

Mother believed in
telling stories.

71.

The blade I've turned
on my own father
draws instant blood.

Whatever changed his course
    — my words
      or Mother's memory —
he's hurtling down
an entirely new path
before he's even sure
where he's headed.

        If you insist on this story —

— the truth.

He's still off-balance,
a composition
with no focal point.
He's all first fire;
I want to see the end result.

Don't just sketch.
Paint a masterpiece.

The state of my purity
on display
for all the world to judge

and yet

my father is willing
to take such action
in my defense.

A trial?

He scowls.

Trial or silence,
make your decision.
Agostino is no fool.
He is already sowing his
seeds.

And finish this damn
painting.

306

Righteous

Shall we finish our story tonight, love? Perhaps. But I do not want to rush these tales. You will not hear them elsewhere. You will not hear them the way I tell them.

Others will tell you Daniel saved Susanna's life. But hear this: Susanna used her voice. She spoke her truth. She could not expect her words to change a single heart, but neither could she be silent.

Her words saved her life.

Where our story picks up tonight, our young, respected leader Daniel happens on the scene and stops the crowd, inquires after Susanna's crime. He does not take Susanna's side immediately, but calls for more investigation before a woman's skull is crushed.

The necessary parties gather. Susanna waits as Daniel questions first the men.

(Always first the men, my love.)

This feels like justice — or at least the possibility of justice. But for Susanna, it's nothing more than prolonged agony. When has Susanna ever seen a man rule in favor of a woman, and against two elders of standing? Most likely all Daniel does is stay Susanna's execution, while casting light on his own wisdom.

But at the very least, Daniel's intervention gives Susanna a few more moments to sit and hold her sister's hand. The sister she sent away.

When finally Susanna is called inside Daniel's chambers, her sister is left to wait outside. Rebecca protests, loath to leave her sister unattended again. But Susanna has faced far worse than one who seeks the truth.

"Your honor." She bows low.

"Please. Speak freely." He acts as though they are equal. And why not? He stands to lose nothing. They both understand perfectly well she will never be his equal.

"I have the highest regard for your husband," he says.

"And for me?" It slips out before she can stop it.

He could dismiss her then and there. Instead he smiles. "You are immensely brave, if nothing else."

Susanna is so brave her hands tremble at her side. But then, to be so terrified and still persist is true courage. Daniel sees all of this.

"The way you spoke to that crowd, rocks already in their hands. You're either brave or mad."

Susanna cannot stand to hold back any longer. "The truth is this: your elders threatened me if I did not disrobe and allow them their pleasures."

"And did you? Faced with a crowd holding stones, many would proclaim their innocence."

Righteous anger blooms; color rises in Susanna's cheeks. Should she show him how this accusation makes her feel and be discounted as hysterical? But if she doesn't, how is he to know the truth?

"They intended to violate me. To seize by force what is not theirs."

He nods, as though she has just explained the state of the olive harvest. "I understand. But now you are faced with a new ordeal, new violations. At worst, you will still be stoned. At best, the accusations against your virtue will continue. This won't end here, regardless of my ruling."

(Though here is what he does not say: if he should rule against Susanna, send her to her death, the matter will end for her accusers. They will go on about their lives, affirmed in their right to take what they want from a woman, no matter the cost to her.)

Susanna's words suggest more confidence than she truly feels. "I know what I am."

Daniel takes that in. A report on stores of grain. "I have questioned your accusers thoroughly."

Susanna dies a thousand deaths in the pause that follows. He has questioned the elders. They have told their story. He upholds their version. What will become of her sister when Susanna is gone and the family honor disgraced?

But Daniel goes on, selecting his words like a lover choosing the finest fig to bestow on his beloved. "There were . . . inconsistencies in their stories. One said your faithlessness occurred beneath an oak tree, the other said a willow."

Susanna's brain scrambles to make sense of Daniel's words. One man described an oak tree, the other a willow. And if they'd both said oak? How would that change the validity of her story?

Exasperated, Daniel furrows his brow, speaks as though she is a child. "I'm ruling in your favor. Both elders will be stoned."

Susanna knows she should be grateful. He has spared her life, after all. And yet —

"What if they'd both told the same lie?"

Daniel is done treating her as though she is a child. Now she has exhausted his patience. "By God's grace, justice prevails for the righteous."

"God's grace? By my strength I did not let them violate me!"

"That is my ruling, which spares your life. Next time, though? You might be more aware of who's watching you bathe."

72.

Trial or silence,
light or shadow.
Sharp edge that draws the eye
or blended lines that lead off
of the canvas.

Lay my heart out bare
or let it devour me
from the inside.

I pick up a paintbrush,
roll it between my fingers.
This is how I tell a story.
Facial expressions
and hands. But words
have never been my friends.

I told my story.

As though it's that simple.
As though Susanna's life

were not at stake.

Somehow I cannot
lift the brush.
The empty canvas mocks me.

But telling a story
in a courtroom,
to a judge,
to people ready
to hear only one thing . . .

What's the point?

I cannot tell if Judith agrees
or only plays
the other side.

Restitution for your father?

He's the one to bring a case,
girl as damaged property,
a painting ruined in a flood.

The court's concerned,
     as always,
          with the men.

What if he's punished?

I don't know how Susanna
can ask that.

Does that change anything?
Did it change anything for you?

She cannot claim it did.
Her violators' deaths
changed nothing
of the stain they'd left
upon her heart.

But Judith never minces words.

As long as Agostino
walks the streets,
he'll keep on taking

what he wants.

It's true.

But will I be forced
to bear the weight
of his every choice
from this moment on?

You're the one who said
it was pointless.

> *That's not what I said.*
> *Here's my real question:*
> *What do you hope to get*
> *out of it?*

73.

Giulio hollers up the stairs,
his voice singsong, delighted.
For the briefest moment
I think my smallest brother
has remembered
he has a sister
he might cherish.

But no.

I descend to see
my brothers, slack-jawed
at the men who loom
in our doorway
all power and
education and
might.

We've come to take
Signorina Gentileschi's
testimony.

317

The thought of strangers — men
in my home without my father
has me unmoored, stuttering and
wordless.

Francesco speaks for me.

> *Don't mind her*
> *You know how girls can be.*

The younger man winks
at my brothers.

> *Girls are trouble, no?*

Giulio puffs up.

> *She just likes attention.*

The man chuckles, nods,
and welcomes Giulio
to the brotherhood.

74.

I am alone
with two men
who'd sooner scorn the Pope
than validate a woman.

My audience,
though not the one I longed for.
I have to pray
the worst outcome
will be that they don't listen,
they won't see.

I tell my story once

          and then again

                    and then again.

The men are either simple,
or they hope to wear me down
until I say:

You're right,
this never happened.
What am I to do
with such a faulty brain?

I do not oblige.
My voice grows thin;
my story doesn't waver.
I paint the blood
they do not want to see.
If I must bear the wounds
then they can stand to look
upon them for a moment.
They'll have the luxury
of forgetting.

When they have seen enough,
I do not show them out.
If my brothers want
so desperately to be
these men, then they can
bid farewell to
my interrogators.

When I am sure
the threat of tears has passed
I step out of the kitchen.
My brothers shuffle growing feet,
find interest in a crack
upon the tiles.
They'll never look me
in the eye again.

75.

The house falls into deepest shadow.
Tuzia never calls for dinner.
Her absence gnaws
away at one last shred of hope
I'd hoarded, one last sense
that someone in this house
could ever understand.

If Tuzia failed to spread
a meal before the hordes
on any other evening
my brothers would have
pounded down the studio door,
demanded food from me.

They do not come.
When finally I hear the door
it's Father, not the closest thing to
     mother
that I've known since I was twelve.

(Always just a shade
too dark, too light,
but close enough to sketch
a guess at might have been.)

Tuzia will not return.

76.

He cannot truly think
I'll be content
with no more explanation
for the disappearance
of the only other woman
in this house.

> *You do not want to*
> *know.*

I do.

He sighs.
These last few months
have aged him more
than all the years
since Mother died.

> *She was paid.*

I blink, uncomprehending.

Tuzia was paid
to look the other way.

Paid by who?

He examines
a scuff on the ground,
finally meets my eye
for the briefest instant.
He can't bear to say
and doesn't need to.
I know.

He turns to go.

But Father —

I won't have her here.
We'll find a way
to muddle through.

77.

Each time I think
it can't get worse
another log is thrown
onto the fire
and the blaze transforms
still more of my life
to ashes.

Tuzia,
with whom I shared
a room, a cycle,
the burden of womanhood,
was never going to be
my Abra.

My fault, perhaps?
I wasn't Judith,
didn't have the grace
to treat her as an equal
when it mattered.

But why could she not see
my disregard,
my irritation, distance
for what they were —
the armor necessary to survive.
She wore it too.
We could have soldiered
on together.

But now I know
the only fighters
in my regiment

    are made of pigment, oil, sweat.

78.

From first fire
to finished masterpiece
takes many months,
even years.
The steps are endless,
fill every waking moment,
now and then intruding
into sleep as well.
Even with the steps
complete, the paint
will not be fully dry
for years, remaining
vulnerable to whatever
may press up against it,
force its will.

And so too, it seems,
a defloration trial.

I was a fool to think
they would hear my story,

make a ruling,
bring the ordeal
to an end.

No, there are months
of interviews,
lists of witnesses,
lines drawn
in the sand,
the whole of Roman art
divided by their loyalties.

On one side:

a nearly penniless,
untrained artist
of the fairer sex,
with the reputation
that comes of being
female in a world
consumed by men.

And on the other:

a savvy, charming con man
formed of lies and sordid history.
But history is nothing
when overshadowed
by a razor tongue
and wealthy benefactors who decide
to profit off a scandal.

79.

Each day
I think
we might
have word
of progress
toward a ruling.

Each day I am mistaken.

My father rages through the house,
ignores our few commissions.

I do not breathe a word of discontent.
Inertia and uncertainty
ignite that piece of me
lain dormant for so long.

I paint again.
Not anything that matters.
The work my father's been ignoring.
Studies to improve my skills.
I must accomplish something.

80.

A pinpoint of light
on a pitch-black canvas:

> Giovanni Stiattesi
> comes to call.

He's Tino's friend,
but also Father's.
He has a daughter,
a lens through which to see
our situation
as something more
than scandal.

> (Why, though, does it take
> a mother, daughter, sister
> for men to take
> a woman at her word?)

There are some things
he thought we ought to know

before it all spills out at trial.

Before he came to Rome,
Agostino Tassi was abandoned
by his wife.

(This is news to Father.
Not to me.)

Upon investigation it seems
Tino's wife fled
when he raped her sister —
a girl of just thirteen.
And then
 (it's not been proven
 but Giovan's heard Tino brag)
he sent a man to find and kill
his wife.

81.

Father's voice is muffled
as I shut myself inside the pantry
once again.
He thanks Signor Stiattesi,
sees this as a seed of hope.
If incest,
      rape,
          and murder
make up Agostino's legacy,
my honor could be heralded,
and his destroyed forever.

But also:

     I was always just a thing.

Any lingering hope I had,
any gasping dream
that somehow
I was special,
somehow so alluring

he could not control his need,
somehow the golden moments
that we shared were genuine
and not just rusted tin
disguised with cheapest paint,
all remnants of this version
of my story
are scraped off the canvas
with Signor Stiattesi's knife.

82.

In the foreground,
the party wronged,
his property damaged,
its provenance questioned,

before the judge,
bestowed by the Church
with the power to rule
on what stays in shadow
and what becomes light.

The middle ground,
composed of witnesses
to a crime committed
behind closed doors,
each with an opinion
on where the eye should fall.

The background:

    the property in question.

83.

I am
a whore,
insatiable,
per Agostino's testimony.

It matters not
that I've repeated
time and again,
        my father's said as well,
if you do not count
the act of violence
against me,
I am a virgin still.

No.

Per the court,
I am a slut.
My studio is less for painting
than for vulgar rendezvous
with any who should wander in

and fall upon my open legs.

They even display letters
evidently sent by me
to countless gentlemen,
        declaring love
        peddling wares.
Never mind I cannot write a word.

An abridged list
of men who've had me
on my back:

        Giovanni Battista Stiattesi
        Geronimo Modenese
        Francesco Scarpellino
        Arigenio, the cleric
        Pasquino Fiorentino
                (Quite convenient
                Signor Fiorentino is now dead
                and therefore cannot
                deny our supposed fling.)

Oh yes, there is one more,
aside from Signor Tassi,
who at first insisted
we'd never lain together,
then changed his tune
to say I'd lain with all the world.

Most damning
(most ridiculous):
my father.

He caps the list of names,
a final polish on Tino's
sculpture carved from lies.

I cannot be satisfied
with all the men of Rome,
and so they say I've had my father, too.

84.

Weeks drag
into months drag
into a numbing sense of time.

Signor Tassi and his thugs perform
as though each day is Carnival
and show no signs of wearing out.
Distract with showy costumes,
shed one mask for another.
Their stories change
like Tiber waters
in a gusty storm.

Still the judge
cannot discern the truth.
Because my word
is not enough
the judge declares
he must have proof —
of what I am not sure.

Two midwives
come before the court.
They bow their heads, submissive,
but they are experts in a field
where women hold the reins.

My mind distracted
by the shiny notion
of a world where only women rule,
I do not hear
the judge's words,
instructions to the midwives.

But then our counsel
prods my elbow,
pushes me to stand,
stumble after the women
to a room
(accompanied by the notary,
a look of glee upon his face
that makes my stomach turn —
I've seen this look before
on men who watch a woman

in a garden, bathing,
just before they demand
she lower her robe).

The only grace:
the judge remains in chambers
to pal around with Tino and his cronies.

Two women
push me on my back,
hoist skirts up to my waist,
and shove their hands inside.

Panic rises.

I am within a court of law.
I should be safe
and yet
it's happening again.

Perhaps
it never stopped.

85.

       We're here.
Susanna.

Judith's hand
smooths my hair
while coarse women
use coarser language
to pry me open,
debate the state of my sex.

       Those men.
Judith whispers,
breath hot in my ear.
       These women who dare
       to judge
       your heart
       by your body
       will never have
       an ounce of your worth.

I summon everything I've got

to keep the tears from flowing.
If I thought women
would show compassion
simply because
we share a place
in this world,
I was a fool.
I am a fool.

Darling girl.
Susanna knows.
Susanna was surrounded
by women who did not help.
We're here.

They stay.
I mirror Judith's stoic face,
match Susanna breath for breath.

And when the midwives
snap at me to make myself
presentable,
I do not tell them

where I wish they'd stick
their pointy tools.

86.

When we emerge,
the men share filthy jokes
behind their hands
as though they care
if I should hear.

The first midwife
before the judge
presents her case:
she's been a midwife
for eleven years,
lest anyone should
question her authority.
After thorough examination
of my *pudenda,*

> (when I ask, Father tells me it
> comes from the Latin word for
> "shame")

She declares I am no virgin.

My hymen,
ruined, like
my reputation.

Was there a question
that my hymen's ruined?
That's what I've told the court
repeatedly.

The next midwife
will not be overshadowed.
She has known pudendas now
for fifteen years.
She confirms the broken hymen,
points out it wasn't
broken recently.

All this is said
as though it proves
that I'm a whore.

But can't it prove
the act of violence
against me?

87.

The judge peers down a nose
so conspicuous it would require
an artist unusually skilled
at perspective to do him justice.

I've told the truth.
I've offered up my body.
There's nothing else to do.

He sighs.
The petulant child
forever whines
      (as though I've lost
      a ball
      a doll
      a game of dice
      and not
      my honor).

Signorina Gentileschi,
are you aware

of what will happen
should you continue to insist
on these accusations?

I'd hoped
the court would
take the time
to study every nuance,
every brushstroke.

I will have no choice
but to subject you to . . .
tests.
Tests of your integrity.

My integrity must be tested
while Agostino smirks,
a man who raped
his wife,
her sister,
possibly even
had them killed.

I will my voice not to tremble.

My integrity can
withstand your tests.

Now the judge
is the one who smirks.

> *I wouldn't be so flippant*
> *if I were you.*
> *We tend to use the manner*
> *most effective for*
>
> *drawing out*
> *the witness.*

I cannot fathom
what that means.
Though Agostino paints
over my words they still
remain, indelible.

I've spoken truth

for many months.
My statement will remain the same.

> *This is not for the pleasure*
> *of the court, of course,*
> *but to clear your name.*
> *To remove any*
> *trace of doubt about*
> *your virtue.*

This time I say nothing.
He has not asked a question.
I do not know what he expects —
  for me to change my story
  now that he makes threats
  I cannot even comprehend?

> *Obstinacy, my child,*
> *could cost you your hands.*

For the first time
in seven months
the courtroom is silent.

Each person watching
knows I'm nothing
without my hands.

What about my hands?

You shall undergo the sibyl.

88.

Look at the sibyls.

Inside the Sistine Chapel,
I could not focus.
Tiptoes only disappointed —
I'd never be close enough.

But Mother crouched down
to match my height,
took my hand, outstretched our arms,
and we gazed along the same sight line
at women on the ceiling.

Look at the sibyls, love.

Five women sit in judgment,
spread across the heavens.

Women who speak truth.
And listen to me, love.
When a woman risks

her place, her very life to speak
a truth the world despises?
Believe her. Always.

The Delphic sibyl
watches Judith
on the ceiling next to her.
The prophetess bears witness
as the warrior slays Holofernes.
If Judith withstood
the sibyl's truth
then I can too.

89.

The ancient sibyls spoke the truth.
And so,
in my courtroom,
will you.
Your arms shall cross
before your breast, my dear,
cords slipped
between each finger
and around your hands,
tightened with a running string.
Your joints will be crushed
with each turn of the garrotte.
It won't take long
to render
your hands
useless.

The judge's final word

reverberates,
almost loud enough
to drown out
Father's gasp.

I cannot bear
to turn and see his face.
I've no idea
what my own
must show.
Horror, shock,
          perhaps.
More likely
pure confusion.

I've followed
Susanna's strokes —
she sent her monsters
to their slaughter.

But I am not to be Susanna.

You don't have to be Susanna.

And so I must be Judith.
My voice will shake
if I should speak
but still I paint the blood.

And what torture
will Signor Tassi undergo?

He snickers —
not the judge,
but the man who tore
my world apart
upon a whim,
an urge,
a bit of wounded pride.

The judge clears his throat,
exchanges glances
with Signor Tassi's counsel.

This trial is torture enough.

90.

Here are my hands.
Do what you will.

PART V

PART V

91.

The bandages wrap once and twice,
three times around my hands.
Barely hands now, though.
Just bits of muscle, sinew, bone.
If I should rip the bandage with my
    teeth,
yank it from my flesh,
what's left would
shrivel to nothing
on the floor.

My brothers turn their eyes away
the moment we walk in.
The house is deadly quiet
without Tuzia's constant songs.

There's only one thing on my mind.
It's not the searing pain
through every joint
and muscle
in my hands.

Or when I cried out
in the courtroom
like a child.

It's true,
it's true,
it's true!

It's not my father's
anguished howl
upon the sound
of crunching bones.

Or even when I found
the breath
the guts
to hold my teacher's gaze
and say before the torture
stole my voice:

This is the ring you give me.
These are your promises.

That's all done.
The only thing that matters now:

Can I still paint?

92.

Nineteen bones
in the human hand,
each more delicate
than the next.
No way to say now
how many jagged splinters
are held together only
by my skin.

Twelve steps
up to the studio,
each one steeper
than the last.
No way to say
if I will reach the summit
but I will not do so
with my father's help.

One girl who climbs alone.

Head spins
stomach roils
skin crawls
as I reach the top.

I make it to my stool
but I can only clamp
a brush between both hands,
a rodent desperately clinging
to a bit of trash.

Ignoring searing pain,
I lean forward
with the tightest grip I can,
determined more than ever
to make my mark.

My arms tremble
from the effort
but somehow, some way,
I get the brush
into the nearest pot of paint.

I grip again,
fight the fire
of someone ripping
off my fingers
one by one.

I persist,
Judith slicing through a neck,
and wrench my arms
toward canvas.

Before I reach my goal,
the paintbrush drops.

The rage simmers.
If I could,
I'd grab a pot of turpentine
to throw   across   the   room.
But even that I cannot do.

Instead I crouch,
retrieve the brush
in rodent claws again.

I jam it toward the canvas,
clumsy as a toddler.
I call it progress.

But when it drops
a third time,
I drop too.
What is the point?

Then Judith's there
beside me on my knees.

That's my girl.

They crushed my hands.

Only your hands.

My hands are my life.
I need them to —

You'll paint again.

She doesn't understand.

367

There's no telling.
I might have given up my only gift,
and all for what?
The desperate hope
that someone might believe me?

      Listen to me, Artemisia.
      Your hands are not your life.
      Your gift does not flow
      from these bones and
          tendons.
      They could slice off your
          hands
      and you would still
      find a way to paint.

      You may have to let the
          bones
      grow back together,
      to let the wounds close.
      But the body is its own
      amazing piece of art.

      It will heal, in time.

368

Broken

A story only shows one moment in time. A few moments. Susanna is threatened, Susanna is accused, Susanna is vindicated.

But push further. Yes, Susanna's story is upheld as the truth. Few women can say that. And Susanna does not bear the wounds she might if things had gone another way. But when she emerges from Daniel's chamber, she fully understands things she didn't before. She will never be the same again.

All Rebecca sees, though, is her sister unbound, walking free. The elder sister shrieks her relief, drops to the floor.

(My boys are dear, but, oh, I wish for you a sister, love.)

Susanna has had enough drama for one day. She pulls her sister up. "Please, let's go home. He has ruled in my favor."

Rebecca sobs, forces her sister to look her in the eyes. "You do not brush me off this time. You hear me, Susanna. In the same situation, two men upon me, I would have succumbed. Yet you —"

Susanna does not want to be a hero. She only told the truth. Another woman might have made another choice. Another would have had no choice at all.

"You would have done whatever you had to do to survive the moment. And you would have received no judgment from me either way, do you understand?"

Rebecca presses a tearstained cheek to her sister's weary shoulder. "It's over," she murmurs.

But people wait outside, people who hours before were prepared to hurl stones at Susanna's head, the families of two men who will be put to death tomorrow. This is far from over.

Susanna gives her sister a task she can seize upon. "Am I presentable?" she asks.

Rebecca smooths her sister's hair. "We'll

need to be up early for the stoning," she says as she fusses at a smudge of dirt on Susanna's sleeve.

Susanna shakes her off. "I'm not going."

Rebecca's face betrays more shock than when the thugs arrived to haul her sister away to be stoned. "Of course you're going. Those two lechers will be stoned because of what you did! You have to —"

"They'll be stoned because of what they did."

(This is so important, love. They'll be stoned because of what they did.)

But Susanna knows she will spend the rest of her life reliving this, explaining this.

"I'm going," huffs Rebecca, smoothing her own hair. "I'm going to watch them die and know you're safe."

But Susanna isn't safe. She is one willow tree away from being smashed in the head with rocks.

A crowd of people who had known Susanna since she was a little girl would have stood by and watched — cheered even — as they fastened a sack over her head. Not so tight she'd suffocate. Just tight enough she wouldn't see what was coming.

The crowd would have started with pebbles. The kind nasty children throw at birds. When they graduated to stones, the size of a fist or so, it would start to hurt. Crashing blows to the head, a broken nose, perhaps.

Finally a chosen one would pick a rock. Perhaps the victim of her heinous crime — those two elders so wronged when she would not succumb to their demands. They would each heave a rock the size of her very head and hurl it at her, shaking inside her sack, bracing every moment for the worst.

And then the worst would come.

The crowd would walk away, having had its entertainment, her broken skull left as one of so many rocks in a pile.

93.

Fresh blood weeps
through bandages
like tears I cannot shed.

The cloth is gray
and tattered at the edges,
the first blood shed
encrusted black.
Mother would have changed
these cloths by now
but Father's been wrapped up
in trying to convince the world
we're still worth hiring.

Once upon a time
I would have called on Tuzia.

(If buyers think
my work is worth nothing,
at least I know my honor's
worth a scudi, maybe two.)

And so, alone,
I unravel bandages
stuck with blood and grime.
It works at first;
the soiled layers
pile on my lap.
I might imagine
this the monthly detritus
of womanhood.
Except for the searing pain,
                    injustice,
                         rage,
the memory of Tino's sneer
as bones were crushed
to prove what my word could not.

And so I'm back to bloody cloths
again, and just like every time before,
they're mine to bear
because I am a woman.

A woman yes,
but not alone.

Susanna's pure white skirts
swish gently round her legs
as she glides up and sets
a bowl of water at my side.

She kneels and reaches
out her hands
for mine, the shredded
parts of me made plain.

Part of me thinks the moment
her pure white hands
touch my demolished ones
she'll float away,
a feather on a breeze.

That doesn't happen.
I barely feel her fingers
as she guides mine
toward the bowl.
I gasp at water
on my weeping wounds.

To wash the filth away,
the crusted blood and memory,
is insurmountable.

Susanna soldiers on
      soothes
      strokes
      sings a song
I can't make out.

I stare into the murky water
until my tears obscure the view.
Maternal kindness
is a razor-sharp reminder
of what — of who — I do not have
to help me carry this weight.

I weep
      and weep
        and weep
enough to clean away the grime.

Next thing I know

Susanna's wrapping up my hands.
Fresh bandages
soon to be encrusted
by the world.

Once bound,
Susanna takes my hands
in hers.

They will heal.

Breathe

When last we left Bethulia, two women waited to see if their kinsfolk would believe they had accomplished the impossible. They had completed what they set out to do. But push further, remember?

Life goes on in Bethulia. Life that would have ended under Assyrian swords if Judith and Abra hadn't done what women do: risked everything.

On the main road, a child sprawls in the dirt, another child looms over him. The triumphant victor hoists a sword skyward, completely unaware that if his sword were not an olive branch, he'd never have the strength to lift it.

"Your head is mine!" he bellows. The children gathered around all hoot until one among them notices they're not alone.

Grown people spoil every game, and the children scatter at the sight of the women returning home from the market, basket in hand. Nervous giggles, whispers. Even the victor drops his sword and runs. The vanquished child scrambles up from the dirt, the last to realize a genuine threat is upon him.

"It's all right," Judith starts to say, but the child falls in his panic to escape. Judith lunges forward to help, but Abra holds her back, her hand on Judith's arm a constant reminder that she's there. She's never left.

The captain's army scattered too, so many frightened children at the discovery their leader was now without a head. Without Holofernes, the once-mighty Assyrian army was nothing more than flailing limbs without a brain to govern them. Judith had been correct when she told her young love, *We only need to reach their leader.* She takes no pleasure in that now.

(Being in the right is not always the solace you might expect.)

Soon, every person Judith passes on the street has heard the story that made its way through the hills to Judith's village, how all of Israel was saved by an unknown, fearsome warrior. The villagers know Judith is the warrior. They saw the head, her bloodstained hands. The ones who slumbered peacefully that night were told of the head, her bloodstained hands, made more monstrous in the retelling. No one ever looked at her the same.

They never will.

Judith can survive the whispered glances now that the true threat is scattered on the wind. So why then does she bolt upright each night just after drifting off to sleep, sheets drenched with fear, panic rising, certain she feels hot blood on her hands, her face, her breasts?

Why does she struggle for breath, claw at her nightclothes, fight the urge to flee into the night?

When finally exhaustion overtakes her, then Abra screams, flings out an arm, strikes Judith in the bed they share. Or else she weeps throughout the night, a lullaby drowned in a funeral dirge.

They didn't share a bed before. But now, the only chance both women have to make it through each night lies in the other's protection. When panic grips one executioner, the other holds her tight and wills her sister back to here and now. To breathe, to stay, to live.

94.

I breathe.
I stay.
I try to live.

The wounds have healed enough
to peel away the bandages,
stretch out my fingers,
hold a brush.
But cramps seize
my hands
after minutes
at the easel.

I set down the brush,
massage the ache,
and do my best
to ignore the racing of my heart
when boots ascend the stairs.

It isn't Tino,
incarcerated while we await

the judge's ruling.
But my body will always
respond as though
he is the one stomping
up the stairs.
Heart, hands, throat,
terror rising.

Father winces at the sight
of me breathing deeply,
digging nails into my thighs
to trick my brain.

When I am almost sure my heart
will not leap from my chest,
I reach for the brush.
My father is now stuck
with me forever.
I must find a way
to prove useful.

But I can't go on
when he speaks:

The verdict is in.

If it were good news
he would not delay.

Tell me.

> *Your innocence
> has been proclaimed.*

Each instant
preserved on canvas
requires days and weeks and months
   and even years
to tell the truth.
If I should live a thousand lifetimes
I would not have sufficient days
to render my shock in its entirety.
After all I went through,
is it possible I was believed?

> *The family honor
> has been restored.*

But there's more,
a hesitancy in his eyes.

And what of Signor Tassi?

The pause is too long
before he says,

> *Five years banishment from*
> *Rome.*

I wait for a just answer
to everything he took.
If I am innocent,
then he is guilty.
But Father's face
says there is no more.
After seven months of trial
destroying my honor,
my prospects,
my purity,
my hands,
Tino is free to ravage another girl
so long as she's outside Rome.

At least I will not see him, but —

> *It's possible he'll*
> *never leave the city.*

I blink at him
till comprehension dawns.

The Medici.

With their power and wealth
and lust for art,
the richest benefactors in the city
will seize this chance to flaunt
how far they fly above the law.

My father nods.

> *They'll harbor him*
> *inside their villa.*
> *And yet, my dear,*
> *it is a victory.*

A victory!
It's not even a decent failure.
My hands were crushed
and why?
Not even for the knowledge
that I'll never see the man again.

> *He may be able to live in
> Rome,*
> *but he won't be able to
> work.*
> *No one will be able to hire
> him.*

*Do you think that's
what matters to me?*

> *It's what matters to him.*

Five years!

I do not wish to weep
in front of Father.
To give him

cause to view me
as anything but equal.

But tears slip down
like that child's accident
dribbling off the canvas.

My father surges forward,
wraps his arms around me,
pulls my face into his chest.
This is not me.
This is not him.
We are some other
family portrait now,
playing a charade of love, support.
If this were real,
if he had ever cared to shield me
now there'd be no need for tears.

What's more, the panic
surges anew
against the arms restraining me.

I break free.

> *After five years, he'll be*
> *forgotten.*
> *It's impossible to climb back*
> *onto the kind of path he was*
> *on.*
> *His career is ruined, I assure*
> *you.*

As though I care.

He would never have
made it to the top.
You were a fool to believe in him.

My father ducks his head
and says a thing I've never
heard him say before:

> *I'm sorry.*

He's sorry.
For what?

It's not enough.
The righteous indignation rises,
the need to skewer him with blame.

You're sorry you can't
use him anymore,
give him access to me
in return for —

Artemisia.

He says it again:

I'm sorry.

And then:

I wish I were a stronger man.

I wish he were too.

95.

The labyrinthine
streets and alleys
of our neighborhood
reflect a perfect map of my life.

Twisting, turning
without reason,
steep, unclimbable stairs to nowhere
that might crumble to dust
upon the slightest
shift

      of earth.

Roads I'm not meant
to walk alone
and yet I do.

What does it matter now
if I'm a proper lady,
accompanied, respected?

I dart through narrow alleys,
dodge the contents of a chamber pot
that's overturned above my head,
> the woman in a third-floor
> > window
> too harried to notice an errant
> > girl below
> or else she recognizes me and
> > sends a message
> of my worth.

I chase the swallows
through the streets.
They tangle in laundry
strung between windows;
I tangle in the shredded remnants
of my life. My feet carry me

to the Ponte Sisto,
as though by crossing a bridge
I might escape this life entirely.
But it only leads to another part
of Rome, more twisting, convoluted
paths and alleys,

more of the same
aimless purgatory.

I lean over the bridge's stone balustrade,
stare into the Tiber's waters below.
I watch a piece of trash
    — a love letter or
    bit of wrapping
    from fish in the market,
    it doesn't even matter which —
drift through the water,
grow waterlogged,
then
    sink
beneath the surface.

> *But you are not*
> *so shortsighted.*

Judith's fingers
brush my right hand
as she joins me
on the bridge

to nowhere.

In drowning this horror,
you would also drown your
promise.

What promise?

There's nothing left for me.

On my left, Susanna's hair
whips in the breeze.

There will come a day,
when this horror is not the
only color on your palette.

But that day's not now.
And even if this horror
becomes an accent color —
a smudge of lead white
to highlight a cheekbone,
a bit of yellow ochre
the glint on a sword —

sometimes those are the pigments
that change one's perception
of an entire work of art.

I do not plan to drown.
I do, however, wish
the river would carry me away.
Instead the stagnant Tiber's stench
assaults me with the truth:

There is nowhere to go.

96.

I spend my days sprawled
on the floor, one
with the dust.
I shall live in my father's house forever,
my dreams of painting thwarted,
feeling sorry for myself.

I ignore the toe
that prods my side.
It's not my father.
(He's given up.)

> *What progress can you make*
> *from that position?*

I'm visualizing painting.
It's the first step.
You don't know.

Judith sighs.

I do not know painting.
I do know something of pain.

I roll my eyes.
We've trod this road before.
Even Judith must have had her moments
when she realized life
would never be the same.
But I have no energy to argue.

My father enters, whisper soft.
He's learned to quiet his approach
and treats me like a woodland creature.

He makes no comment
on the state of the studio
or my current position.
He simply sits on the ground
at my side.

We need to discuss your hand.

I hold both hands up,

demonstrate their flexibility.

They're nearly healed.

> *I meant your marriage*
> *prospects.*

This is new.

I have no marriage prospects.

> *That isn't so.*
> *The family's honor was*
> *restored.*
> *You can marry.*

No one will have me.

It's cruel even to suggest.

> *Not here, in Rome.*
> *But you'll be safer in Florence.*
> *You'll marry Pierantonio*
> *Stiattesi.*

I sit up with a jolt,
ignore the rush of blood to my brain.

Stiattesi?

Giovanni arranged it.

Giovanni Stiattesi,
named in the trial
as one of my paramours.
Agostino's friend
who stood and spoke
instead in my defense.
Whose testimony held
more weight than my own,
not because he bore witness
the day Tino held me down
and made me bleed
but because he is a man.

As decent as Giovanni is,
I've no way to know
who his relation may be.

You expect me to go through
with a marriage of your arrangement?
You, who kept me locked
in the studio to be assaulted
by your friend?

My father lets out a huff of frustration,
with me or with himself, I cannot tell.

> *Giovan's brother is a painter,*
> *He can't afford a proper wife,*
> *but he'll take you.*

I cannot help but laugh.
It comes out as a strangled bark.

A penniless hack!
How generous of you.

> *You'll get out of this city,*
> *away from the scandal.*
> *His family is a direct ticket*
> *into Florentine society.*

Honestly, Artemisia,
it's more than I could have done
here.
You'll have an audience for your
art.
You'll have your own studio.

It is ultimately your choice,
but as I see it,
you have no other.

97.

I take a length of cloth
and hold it to my head —
   a wedding veil.

I do not regret the days of make-believe,
but for every time I played at bride
I should have played at goddess
      river
       warrior queen.

Those childhood stories
ending in a grand wedding
are incomplete, their heroines left
to tangle in their veils forever.

Judith pulls the cloth from my hand
and spreads it on the ground.

  Not a bridal veil. A canvas.

Susanna smooths

the wrinkles in the cloth.

And not a shield. A weapon.

They tell me I know
about perspective now.
Too well.
They say I'm standing
at the start of a long road,
looking out into the distance.
What do I see?

I can't know.

You'll paint a masterpiece.

Judith gathers paints,
pulls me to my knees.

On the floor?

*You must have done this
when you were a child.*

Father would have killed me.

> *Your father doesn't say*
> *how you paint now.*

My hands are still broken.

> *All of you is broken.*

> *We understand.*

Judith takes one of my hands,
Susanna takes the other.
They plunge my fingers into paint,
smear them across
the outstretched cloth.

This is madness.
And yet the paint flowing
straight from skin to canvas
feels more precisely right
than anything I've ever done before.

One day, this will all
recede into the background,
underpainting
giving texture to
the master's strokes,
and I, the master.

98.

When I am clean,
just after a scrubbing,
a part of myself is missing,
like a severed limb,
a skeleton with no muscles,
a corpse.

I am not myself unless
some part of my body
is covered in paint.
The more paint, the more cover,
the more I am Artemisia.

The paint is not a shield
or armor
but another skin.

And even if it's scrubbed away,
there's paint inside,
pounding through my veins.

Perhaps I don't have blood at all.
Not really.
Only paint.
Perfectly pure
ruby red paint
flowing straight
to my heart:
    my canvas.

99.

I will show you
what a woman can do.

100.

Everything begins from here:
the viewing point,

the place where you stand,
your eye level.

That single point on the horizon
where all other lines
                    converge.

Afterword

Artemisia Gentileschi was born in Rome on July 8, 1593, and died somewhere between 1654 and 1656. More than fifty of her paintings and the three-hundred-page transcript of the 1611 trial depicted in this novel survive to this day. You can read the transcript in Mary D. Garrard's excellent book, *Artemisia Gentileschi* (Princeton University Press), to which I owe an enormous debt.

Artemisia had one daughter, whom she named Prudentia, after her mother. She trained her daughter to paint.

Acknowledgments

I wrote many books and endured rather stunning numbers of rejections on my road to publication. I truly feel those years of heartache and trunked manuscripts were entirely worth it, if they meant I would one day get to entrust my work to Andrew Karre. I am deeply in awe of his intellect, his relentless dedication to fearless storytelling, and the thoughtful care with which he has shepherded my heart book to publication.

My agent, Jim McCarthy, is the kindest, most insightful, and most truly hilarious person I could ever have dreamed up to guide me on this publishing journey. I wouldn't have adapted *Blood Water Paint* into a novel without his encouragement to do so, and I am forever indebted to him

413

for finding it a perfect home at Dutton.

Thank you to the wonderful team at Dutton Books for Young Readers for their skill, passion, and dedication in bringing this book to publication. It takes a lot of people to make some words in a file into a book you can hold in your hands. Thank you, Julie Strauss-Gabel, Melissa Faulner, Natalie Vielkind, Anna Booth, Theresa Evangelista, Rosanne Lauer, Amy Schneider, Janet Rosenberg, and Katie Quinn.

I do not know how Artemisia survived the artist's road without the support of other female artists. I have been unbelievably blessed to be bolstered along my journey by amazing friends and critique partners. Jessica Lawson was the first, and she has been there ever since with hilarious email titles, enthusiastic cheerleading, and the deepest kind of friendship. I am also indebted to the following women, for their friendship and their wise input on *Blood Water Paint:* Amy Elizabeth Bishop, Sharon Roat, Laura Shovan, Amanda Rawson Hill, Ellie Terry, Kip Campbell, Mel Stephenson, and Alexandra Alessandri.

I am also beholden for the love and support of my writing friends who lift me up, commiserate, and let me vent. Much love to Rachel Lynn Solomon, Tara Dairman, Ann Bedichek Braden, and Brent Taylor. Also buckets of gratitude to Brenda Drake and the entire Pitchwars family.

Blood Water Paint is the tenth novel I wrote. I cannot possibly list all the people who have given me feedback and support since the beginning. But if you ever read one of my manuscripts or query letters, or gave me a pep talk, or celebrated a milestone with me, you contributed to my growth as a writer. I am head over heels in love with my writing community, which has included Absolute Write, Pitchwars, Project Mayhem, the Electric Eighteens, the Class of 2K18, and kidlit Twitter.

Blood Water Paint began as a play. It had an extremely long development process, which culminated in its world premiere production at Live Girls Theater in 2015. I am forever indebted to my theatrical soul mate, director Amy Poisson, and the utterly fearless artistic director of Live Girls, Meghan Arnette, for their belief in Artemisia's story. Thank you also to the sublime cast and stellar designers, whose work I went back to many times in my mind as I worked on the book.

My family has supported my creativity from the time I was a child. Thank you to my father, who took me to the bookstore (and ice-cream shop) every Saturday morning. Thank you, Mom and Dana, for always being there for absolutely everything. Thank you to my sister Jennifer. I love you more than I can say.

And finally, I will never have sufficient words to thank my husband, Mariño, and my children, Cordelia and Joaquín, who accept the fact that I rarely get out of pajamas, the house is never clean, and every single time I put water on to boil, I forget it's on the stove. You are my everything. And without you, the house would burn down.

Resources

You may recognize yourself in parts of Artemisia's story in much the same way Artemisia recognized herself in Susanna's and Judith's stories. Sometimes it feels like little has changed. But there are resources available to today's survivors of sexual violence.

I believe, like Artemisia's mother, in telling stories. Whatever your story, I hope you tell it to someone when you're ready. There's power in the telling.

Among the organizations dedicated to helping survivors of sexual violence are the National Sexual Violence Resource Center (www.nsvrc.org) and Rape, Abuse, and Incest National Network, better known as RAINN (www.rainn.org). If you would like to speak confidentially with someone trained to hear your story, you can call 800-656-HOPE (4673).

You are not alone.

ABOUT THE AUTHOR

Joy McCullough writes books and plays from her home in the Seattle area, where she lives with her husband and two children. She studied theater at Northwestern University, fell in love with her husband atop a Guatemalan volcano, and now spends her days surrounded by books and kids and chocolate. *Blood Water Paint* is her debut novel.

The employees of Thorndike Press hope you have enjoyed this Large Print book. All our Thorndike, Wheeler, and Kennebec Large Print titles are designed for easy reading, and all our books are made to last. Other Thorndike Press Large Print books are available at your library, through selected bookstores, or directly from us.

For information about titles, please call:
   (800) 223-1244

or visit our Web site at:
   http://gale.cengage.com/thorndike

To share your comments, please write:
   Publisher
   Thorndike Press
   10 Water St., Suite 310
   Waterville, ME 04901